SOMETHING ELSE

A STORY OF HOPE

NOVEL BY
DYRRELL MANGALSINGH

SOMETHING ELSE

A STORY OF HOPE

ReadersMagnet, LLC

TABLE OF CONTENTS

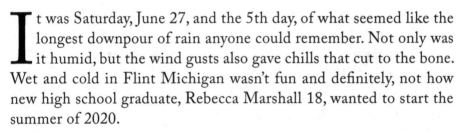

It was Saturday, June 27, and the 5th day, of what seemed like the longest downpour of rain anyone could remember. Not only was it humid, but the wind gusts also gave chills that cut to the bone. Wet and cold in Flint Michigan wasn't fun and definitely, not how new high school graduate, Rebecca Marshall 18, wanted to start the summer of 2020.

Rebecca is a pretty, 5' 6" 110lb soaking wet tomboy. A bit of a smartass, with a genuine heart of gold. Her pleasant disposition and charm gravitate people towards her. Despite being born with a deformed left arm, she goes about life with confidence that nothing is going to get in her way...all except, Mother Nature. She lays curled up in a blanket, on the living room couch that was almost as comfortable as her bed. The couch was in a house, passed down to her mother. It's a quaint one-story, 4bedroom Victorian-style house built in the 1950s, with a small front porch. The walls are filled with family pictures of George and Mary and the kids. There is a china cabinet with Grandma Mary's treasured china and spread throughout the house are mementos of her uncles and grandparents. She flips through the muted TV stations aimlessly, praying for some random familiar programming to catch her eye and hold her attention if only briefly. Most stations have Michigan's Governor Joshua Finley giving PSA warnings for heavy rain and flooding. The governor was a distant cousin to her mother Maggie, whom Rebecca only met once at a family reunion ten years ago. She remembers him as a nice guy, she mostly remembers the distinct patch of grey hair on the side of his head. It made him look funny to her. She keeps clicking away on the remote. Normally, watching movies would be fine to her, Rebecca could watch them all day. She was such a huge movie buff, and she'd randomly quote movie lines when she spoke. But this was not how she planned to start her summer vacation. The rain was ruining everything. Silently she murmurs, "It can't rain all the time."

From down the hall, she hears an energetic teen, voicing ill discontents to his online adversary, along with the hectic sounds of a joystick and slams of arcade buttons deep in combat delivering fierce blows. "Jordan keep it down in there!" Rebecca yells. "I'm one round away from decimating this tardy tard Becca, come watch!" Jordan yells back.

Rebecca slowly gets up and makes her way down the hall peeking in on her little brother. The battle is intense, or as intense as anyone who likes fighting games. She looks on and smiles as he finishes triumphantly. "Becca, did you see? Did you see me make mincemeat of that tard!!?" Jordan joyfully exclaims. Rebecca dotingly says "Yes!! Good job, he never had a chance bro".

Jordan was a happy, beautifully dispositioned kid, even though he suffers from a genetic condition, causing his retinas to degenerate over time. He's 14 and has been completely blind for the majority of his teenage years, but you'd never know that to talk to him. The online players only find out about his handicap, after he annihilates them. He likes nothing better than to boast that a blind kid beat them.

Rebecca walks back to her comfy throne, and whispers, "I see you and I smile little brother." Back to her warm spot she hears the rain coming down even harder. She looks at the grandfather clock that has been in the family for generations, its 5:39 pm, mom should be home from work soon, "SHIT!!" she stammers. Rebecca jumps up, runs to the kitchen, and starts cleaning it from the lunch mess, made hours earlier. You would have thought a family of 10 had eaten for the mess that was displayed. And no sooner the last dish goes into the dishwasher, and the door is shut, the crackling of gravel under tires resonates against the side of the house.

Maggie Marshall 40, pulls up the gravel driveway to the house that sits on five acres of grassland, the perimeter fortified by a barbed-wire fence. Maggie's an RN at the local clinic, she's the nicest, most loving woman you'd ever met… sometimes. Never married, and raising two kids alone, was her choice. Her priority in life was seeing her kids happy and loved.

As she puts the car in park the blasts of the car horn echo through the house. Moments later two heads peer out the back door. The driver's window rolls down just enough so they can hear the yell "Y'all better get your asses out here and help with these groceries!" The sweet woman opens the car door, cursing at the droplets smacking her face. The kids take their positions, Jordan at the back door, and Rebecca the runner, shuttling bags from the car handing them off to Jordan. They had their system. Rebecca even though one-armed, was efficient using her mouth for one bag and right hand for the other.

"Hi Mom, when is it supposed to stop raining?" Jordan says as Maggie enters the house. "Supposedly by morning Jordan, why? Were you going to get up off your butt and get some sunshine?" Maggie says cynically. "Hell No! I got souls to crush mom… but I might go out on the porch, soak up some sun, so I can be the ray of light in your life that you know I am." he chuckles as he says it. Then all three laugh at his cute confidence. Maggie hangs her wet raincoat up in the rack by the back door and starts unpacking the groceries.

chapter one

MAGGIE

The town of Flint had changed throughout the years, once a booming motor vehicle manufacturing city, with a great middle class full of prosperity. Now, with massive layoffs, automotive plant closures, and environmental waste dumping infecting the adjoining rivers. It has made the town, a struggling metropolis for survival.

The townspeople struck with the plight of living in a place that feels all but forgotten, they form fundraisers and apply for government aid to assist in the cleaning and removal of the cancerous waste. This slow process along with dealing with the bureaucracy of a town stripped of its natural resources was frustrating, especially for Hope Flowers.

Hope is a bright, fresh out of high school ambitious 18yr old woman. Tall and thin with fire engine red hair, which also matched her fiery personality. Since she was 15, she has been organizing and trying everything from bake sales, to rallies to draw attention to the crisis in Flint. With her last summer upon before she headed off to Clemson University, she wanted to try her best and muster all the help she could for Flint. Her commitment was admirable, and it was one of the many things that Rebecca loved about her. They met when Hope moved to Flint when she was 8 and they were connected at the hip ever since.

Phone rings, "Hi Hope, this weather sucks soooo." Rebecca gasps. "I know, but it's supposed to be over tomorrow. I was thinking of doing a church potluck with a donation incentive. How about we auction off dates with a few of us newly graduated members of society?" she says with exuberance. 'Do you think your uncle would be on board with something like that? We wouldn't be pimping out his church or anything, I'm just running out of ideas to raise money." "Um, do you even know my Uncle Ed...? He'd think you were the queen harlot herself," Rebecca replies laughingly. "Your uncle is lame…okay fine how about a bake sale then?" Hope says. "Yeah, I'm sure that'll be JC enough, why don't you come over tomorrow, and we can draw up the signs," Rebecca says. "Okay I'll be there bright and not too early, I do like my sleep, you know me…" Hope replied in a chipper manner. "Becca get your butt over here and help with these groceries!" Mom yells. "Hope I gotta go, you know who is cracking the whip." Rebecca reluctantly says. "Okay text me later, bye sis," Hope says. "Okay bye sister," Rebecca says.

Rebecca stomps out of the living room into the kitchen. "Stomp all you want you're still gonna have to put the groceries away. What? You think things magically materialize in the fridge or pantry for you to go get when you want. No, you have to stock it there first. You kids better figure this out soon, I ain't gonna be around forever." Maggie bluntly says. "Mom I'm blind though." Jordan fires with. "No excuse, a place for everything, and everything in its place, my rules and you'll see one day, your rules." Maggie fires back. Maggie looks at both of them sternly but lovingly then turns and walks out of the kitchen to her room to unwind from the day. Jordan even blind, felt the look and as soon as she was gone, he says to his sister "You know that was all directed at you… I'm gonna be rich one day, and I won't have to lift a spoon." Jordan says snidely. "Yeah, well that's great because you're gonna need to be rich, cause you suck at putting away groceries. You're about to put cereal in the freezer, Rockefeller." Rebecca replied. Jordan pauses, then flips the box over his head catching it behind his back with his other hand, does a spin move, then feels his way to the pantry and says, "All on purpose Becca, I'm just making sure you know where everything goes. Nice catch…"

Rebecca smiles as she's emptying the last bag. "Brat" then says softly, 'I see you…"

The rain seems to be dwindling as dusk arrives. The cloud ceiling is extremely low like you could almost reach up and touch them. Rebecca stands out on the porch sipping on some hot chocolate, she listens to the light patter of raindrops on the roof. Their house sits right on the outskirts of town and is nice and quiet, sometimes too quiet, but still better than the noise of downtown. She could also hear the clinging and clanging of pots as her mom makes dinner. It was her favorite, spaghetti and meatballs. Rebecca thought, maybe she should go help her hard-working mother, she takes a sip of cocoa and goes back inside to help.

Rebecca and Maggie worked well together, mostly because Rebecca learned who was running the show a long time ago. But it was not even that, more like an understanding. Growing up without a father, put a lot on Maggie, she had to be a strong role model for her kids. While dishing out love and discipline at the same time, it was not easy. Maggie was a first-generation resident of Flint. Her family moved there in 1970 from New York, when her father George, got a supervisory job at the General Motors Plant. She was born 10yrs later and the youngest of 3. She had two older brothers Ed 51, a minister at a local church, and Pete 48, a geologist professor at Michigan State University. Maggie to say the least was not a planned baby, born in 1980 when times were about to start getting rough in Flint. Her mother Mary never let her feel that though, nor did her father. They made the best with what they had and planned for the kids' education. Moreover, it all worked out, since Ed became a minister his college money went to Pete, and Pete's went to Maggie's nursing degree. It all flowed.

George was not overly caught up in the motor company's cutbacks, his tenure with GM saved him. They gave him a position in Quality Control. This all seemed like a comfortable situation, until July 3rd 1988. George and Mary while driving back home from a friend's house, were broadsided in an intersection by a drunk driver. Mary died instantly, and George died in a coma a week later. The driver a 30yr old male was sentenced to 16yrs in prison. This tragic incident is what guided Ed into dedicating his life to being a voice of God, and forgiveness. Even though the life insurance policy was sufficient, there was family support from grandparents, uncles, and aunts. Ed felt it was his duty being the eldest, to take on the role and raise his little brother and sister. But he came up short, not for the lack of ambition. He just didn't know how, and the more he tried to be like his father George, the more he failed. He was a good man but... to say the truth Pete was more like his father, Ed was more like George's brother Daniel. Who was good, just never good enough, it seemed he was cursed in some way. Everything that George touched went to gold and Daniel more like bronze. Hence, the reason Daniel moved to Canada was far away from facing his shortcomings. And this was exactly what Ed was, he was always in competition with his younger brother. He was never going to win in the way he wanted to. Pete knew that and made excuses to protect his brother from other people. In Pete's eyes, Ed was a hero to him. Eventually, Ed gave up and sought his resolve in the Bible. George's and Mary's parents were given custodial rights, but Ed took over and tried to run the house by the word of the bible. Praying before eating and bed was a must, along with church on Sundays. And in effect, the spiritual reinforcement helped them bond to their dead parents. The family though was not overly religious and in actuality when George was alive, he didn't believe in organized religion. So, where Ed got this idea from, was entirely on him. Ed did do his best to make sure his siblings studied, and always was there to quiz them. And in a way, that made him feel like he guided them to a better life, overlooking and being their caretaker. Now, Ed was a minister in a beautiful church, he had a core congregation that was there every Sunday rain or shine. And then there was the general congregation, who he was slowly losing throughout the years. Not for any other reason than, they had no time for God he thought. But Ed was always there for those that needed a place. That's just the man he was.

Pete was like his father before George had the responsibility of a wife and children, an adventurer. When Pete graduated high school at 18, he took some money from his share of the life insurance and backpacked the world for a year. "I just needed to get away and see the world before college." He would say with a grin on the left side, the same grin his father had. However, it was more than that, he was following up on all the places and things, his father told him about when he was growing up. I guess this made Pete feel connected to his dad, in his own way. When he came back the stories he would tell, would keep Maggie up all night listening. Ed would listen and smile, but life outside Flint never excited him that much. Pete went off to college at the University of California Berkeley, which fit his broad free-spirit disposition. He graduated with a degree in geology and made his way back to Michigan to be around family. Pete was single with prospects. He always wanted to get married and even came close, but for some reason still hadn't finalized the deal to be a family man. Which everyone thought was odd, seeing how great he was to his niece and nephew. Maggie benefitted from this though.

Maggie being the only girl, and a daddy's girl, had all a child could want growing up. Real young, her parents could see her independent will, surfacing. Being raised on 5 acres meant a lot of room to explore. And she did, with her trusted sidekick named Stubborn, a German shepherd/black lab mix, born just a year after Maggie, they were inseparable. After school they'd sit on the porch, and wait for George to come home, it was like Christmas every day. When George and Mary died, it was a significant blow to Maggie. Her brothers and grandparents got her psychiatric help, but what actually helped her through, was Stubborn. She died a month before Christmas in 1997 at the ripe age of 16. Maggie buried her in the forest behind their property, under an oak tree that she carved in "My best friend, my first love". In school, Maggie kept to herself, but her inner being would always seep out. She was a tomboy, and when it came time for competitive sports, she'd always find her way onto the podium. All the kids knew her family background and most were sympathetic. She only got in one fight, and it was with a boy 1yr older in high school. He accused her dad of stealing the job his dad was supposed to have because he was black. The kid knew the second he said it, the outcome was not going to be in his favor. Though short, Maggie was strong and knew how to throw a punch. The boy suffered a broken nose and two black eyes. The story quickly carried throughout the school and town. Ed and Pete put up the front, don't mess with the Marshalls, and from then on people knew not to mess with them. After Maggie graduated, she immersed herself into nursing school.

She rarely made time for friends, mostly she just casually hung out with classmates here and there. There was one particular student that she'd always happen to see at the same parties or hangouts. Trevor Washington 22, handsome, tall, well-built, and second in class after Maggie. They eventually hit it off, and on the night after graduation, Maggie gave herself to him. This however did not work according to plan. Maggie got pregnant, and then Trevor was nowhere to be found. Rumor was he ran off to Hawaii with his family, with no plans on coming back. This was a major blow to Maggie. Ed was dead set against abortion, and Pete was, "It's your choice kiddo I'm here no matter." She felt trapped but she wasn't a quitter, so she made up her mind to tough it out and make it work.

Six months into the pregnancy, the doctors explained, that there might be a complication with the baby's growth. Somehow, the left arm was wrapped around the umbilical cord causing it to restrict growth. The baby was delivered via C-section 2 weeks early. The deformity was worse than described. The baby, Rebecca Mary Marshall, would forever have limited movement in her left arm. Her forearm was curved like an S, this would prove to be just a minor obstacle Rebecca would overcome throughout her childhood, and her essence and vigor would win over most people she met.

The bond between Maggie and Rebecca was instant and without sympathy. As Rebecca was growing up, Maggie could see so much of her in her daughter. The fearlessness and curiosity for life made her so proud and happy she chose to keep her. Her brothers, especially Pete spoiled the hell out of Rebecca. Maggie was given the family house to raise her. Ed lived in a nice cottage behind his church, about a mile away. And Pete lived in a condominium in Lansing Michigan.

Though spoiled Maggie never let Rebecca stray too far, there were rules and they were there to be followed. Maggie taught her everything she could to make up for being a solo parent. Their special time would be Sundays, Maggie would put on her rubber boots, along with Rebecca's matching ones. Then Maggie would put her on her lap, and they would ride the lawnmower they named Caroline, throughout the giant property cutting the grass, laughing, and talking for hours. This only lasted till Rebecca was 10 but it opened the doors of communication. Rebecca looked up to her mom, to her she was a superhero.

Back to the present, Rebecca was slowly stirring the spaghetti, so it didn't stick to the sides and Maggie is chopping vegetables for the salad. "Jordan stop playing games, wash your hands and come help set the table, dinner will be ready in five minutes," Maggie yelled. "Okay, Mom." Jordan bellowed back.

Jordan was born to one of Maggie's recurring teenage visitors to the clinic. Her name was Susan, sadly she was frequently abused physically and mentally, by her father and her boyfriend. She would randomly show up to the clinic with new bruises, and Maggie would tend to her, almost always for free. She befriended Maggie and was probably the only friend she had. She got pregnant while working the street, and gave birth. And a year later, she committed suicide and willed Jordan to Maggie. Jordan was a healthy baby, but a little hard to handle as a toddler. In time with love, he grew out of aggressiveness, unfortunately soon after, he was diagnosed with a degenerative eye disease. Maggie was on pins and needles about how he'd react to the news about his ailment. He was only 11, but Jordan surprised everyone and after a week he embraced his disease. He researched everything and spent many days hiking trails with Rebecca, soaking up what he knew would be the last visual memories. The kid was tough, and Rebecca admired him for his courage. They'd sit and watch the sunset from the hilltops, and even though they were not related by blood they knew they'd always have this connection. As the disease ran its course, hikes became less frequent. On the last one, Rebecca pretty much hand-guided Jordan to the top of the hill, but he didn't complain. He knew… and also knew it would be quick because they'd have to get down before dark. Jordan in appreciation whispered to his sister "I feel you sister, and it makes me smile" and she replied, "I see you brother, and it makes me smile."

The dinner placements were set now, and the house smelt of savory Italian spices. The three sat around the table laughing and poking fun at each other, as the rain finally stopped. It was a happy loving family… they never knew things were about to change, forever.

chapter two

RES

Everyone was sound asleep in the Marshall house. There was a thick fog draped over the landscape, the night was as still as a cat before the pounce. The time was 2:08 am on Sunday, June 28, 2020. Rebecca woke up thirsty, she slowly dragged herself to the kitchen for some water. While drinking her sleepy eyes broke open just enough to see out the kitchen window, the fog nestled in the backyard. She felt like her house was amongst the clouds. Then suddenly, there was a bright flash and then BOOM!!! In the sky miles away. It startled her to the point she almost dropped the glass. It didn't seem to wake the other two occupants in the house. Rebecca looks closer through the window; it looks like everything is standing still and then ZZZZZZIP CRASH!!!! Shocked and stunned she jerks back, but still, eyes focused. It looks like something crashed into the old barn on their property. The barn had been animal-free for years now. Looking on intently, she was hoping maybe whatever hit the barn, would somehow catch it on fire and burn it to the ground. They were planning on tearing it down and hocking all the wood this summer, anyway. This way it would kill two birds, with one meteorite... There was nothing in it of real value anyway, "OH NO Caroline!" she gasped. Rebecca runs to her room, throws on a robe and some sandals, and runs out the backdoor, as quietly as she can. As she approaches the barn through the fog, she feels awkward like there's a monster lurking, waiting to jump out and eat her. What a silly notion she thought, it would be more like little green men "Take me to your leader." she whispered then chuckles. When she gets to the doors it takes her a few tries to slide open. That included her slipping and falling in the wet grass a couple of times, the door was not easy to open with one arm. Once she opened it, inside the barn was not much better than outside. The fog had crept in through broken windows, the barn was a mess, but her mom's lawnmower was okay. Rebecca looked up and could see a huge hole in the roof. The floor of the barn was full of broken hay bales, about three inches deep. They got broken up, the summer prior during a hay fight Rebecca had with her friends. Walking on it, was like walking on a different planet she thought, all mushy and wet from all the rain. Scanning the barn she sees something directly under the hole, it is glowing. Rebecca gets closer, it looks embedded in the ground. She bends down and brushes some of the hay away. It's glowing, and slowly pulsating with a dark purple hue. It was barely peeking out of the ground, no bigger than the top of a large beach ball. Rebecca thought, shouldn't this be hot, it just burned through our atmosphere, the dry straw should be ablaze. She hesitates, and then grimaces at what she was about to do, she reaches her right hand down slowly then flinches it back up. She says to herself, "Why mess up the only good arm I got." She then stretches her left arm as far as it can go, bending over for the rest, till her index finger hovers over the glowing Orb. Seconds rolls by, she feels frozen yet free staring into the pulsing light. Her emotions and senses all feel heightened…and then her finger drops. Instantly Rebecca's heart races, nerves tingle, body clenches with her eyes rolled back. She feels the blood rush to her brain with an overwhelming euphoric feeling, throughout her whole body. She falls to the ground. Breathing heavily she gasps out" OH Shit!! What the hell was that? Oh my god…oh my GOD!" She gets up looks herself over. Everything is the same as it ever was. She looks at the Orb which is still pulsing. Rebecca covers up the Orb with hay, then runs out and shuts the barn door. Walking back, she's trying to come to terms with what she just experienced, she can feel the pulse of the Orb in her, but it's slowly subsiding. She opens the house door, and both housemates are still fast asleep, she can hear her mom snoring.

As she gets back to her room, it feels like the euphoria is wearing off and she is becoming extremely tired. She barely has time to kick off her sandals before she's out for the count.

On this particular night, Rebecca was going to have the most vividly real dream she'd ever had. It starts like this….It's pitch black, she hears soothing voices say, "We are here to help you." She's then floating high up over a landscape full of an assortment of colors, bright and vibrant. The landscape is like earth, with rolling hills and giant mountains in the distance. Similar terrain also with fields of trees and grass, but they are not green, they were variations of light to dark blue. Flying over, she can see a web of hundreds of interlocking green domes, connected by white tunnels that spread over miles of terrain. She sees an ocean mating up to land. The water is yellowish/gold, reflected by an enormous sun that shines white. It looks so foreign and yet familiar at the same time. In an instant, she's zoomed in to one of the giant domes, where she sees them. They moved like humans, some are tall, some shorter, some wide, and some thin. They look like the people of the earth except the skin tone is pure white and their hair is black with solid soft blue eyes. They are all dressed, in a form of summer dresses. Rebecca is led by one of them to a big screen-like television… but now it feels like she's now on the television. It flickers on, and she watches at what seems to be an archive of their history. It's a place like earth, only 1000yrs ahead of earth's current time. She then hears unison voices say "Zan" which is their home planet. A war breaks out in their world. The video keeps playing and she sees small spaceships launching from all parts of the planet. They are fired upon from the surface, and from satellites Orbiting Zan, the voices say "Retaks", they are a race on the planet, leaving destruction in their wake. A scramble ensues of 100 crafts maneuvering for survival, they are no match for the ordnance being hurled at them. One by one they are picked out of space… but in the distance, a thruster burns… one escapes. She then sees the ship arriving at a faraway lush world, and witnesses a time-lapse of community beings flourishing… She hears unison voices again whisper "Remaks." Another race from planet Zan, this race is docile and highly creative. These beings do not have an aura around them but are the same being as she saw at first. Only, they have pinkish skin with blue hair and green eyes. The community is a bunch of scientists, she sees the time-lapse of them building green domes and connecting with the environment and all its inhabitants. The animals there are larger than the earth, and the species she sees are breathtaking. She reaches her hand out to touch what looks like an Elephant mixed with a Panda, and the screen starts fast-forwarding faster. It is now around 1500yrs since they first arrived. She sees the scientist create new species of animals and vegetation. Then, new hybrids of themselves, now have a bright aura surrounding them. The aura glows either red or blue, it appears that the males are blue and females are red. They look like, life in light...she can feel them, and they feel like the first breath of a baby, like a shock of adrenaline, like the clarity of the mind and unlimited energy all at once. Then everything goes black... Rebecca sees the planet from space and hears the unison voices, "Res" the name of their new home planet. Then a black icosahedron-shaped spaceship slowly comes into view and hovers over Res. The voices say, "Retaks". Then all she sees are fires and explosions. Hundreds of tall dark-orange beings are attacking everything in sight. They are not particularly scary looking, just overly aggressive and mean. They are bigger than the Remaks but look similar to them. Red and blue auras are being evaporated instantly, after being shot by the invader's weaponry. Rebecca hears thousands of cries from the Remaks, the sounds are like shrieking children. She is then shown what looks like a giant clear crystal, in the shape of a teardrop about the size of a large television. Then eight Remaks four red auras, and four blue auras align themselves on each side of the teardrop. One by one, each channels its life force essence into the teardrop, leaving eight discarded carcasses on the floor. The clear teardrop has now turned purple, with the combination of red and blue auras. It then launches away from the planet fast as the speed of light. They show her a plotted course to earth, at its current time 1020AD... everything then goes black. She hears something walking towards her. Then a small light shines down, and out of the darkness a Panda Elephant slowly walks up to her, she reaches out again and caresses its furry trunk, it's so soft, and the creature lets out a gentle growl, and nuzzles up against her hand. She laughs, as she realizes that she's using both of her hands. Rebecca looks deep into the animal's big black eyes… and then again everything goes black.

It's 9:35 am, there's a loud crash of pots, and in the kitchen that awakens Rebecca. An apologetic "Sorry, I'm Okay!" comes from her brother in the kitchen. She's slow to get up while getting a bearing of where she's at. She rubs her face and then sits up frantically in bed looking at her hands. Her left arm and hand are just like her right arm and hand. She instantly, uncontrollably starts crying in tears of joy and overwhelmingness. Rebecca can't stop touching and moving her newly found appendage. It's hard to see through her tears, so she keeps rubbing the tears away, then sees her arm and it happens all over again. It's like she never had anything wrong with the arm, ever. Jordan knocks on his sister's door and says, "Becca you okay?" Rebecca replies with restraint, "YES, yes I'm okay brother." She then jumps out of bed looks out her window, it's a bright sunny morning. Runs to her door fling it open with her new hand and screams out "WOOHOOO!" Then runs through the house out the back door. All while her brother is yelling, "You're lucky moms at work, you're not supposed to be running in the house, oh and good morning to you too." She's running so fast she runs out of her sandals. This time she opens the barn door with no problem, the barn is still a mess but as Rebecca gets closer, she sees a small circle of newly grown grass around the purple ball. She brushes the hay away, parts the grass, and just sits looking at her newly discovered visitor. She then says lovingly, "Thank you…" and touches the vessel with her new arm, as a tear rolls down her cheek, the Orb stops pulsing and just glows bright purple.

Rebecca gets back to the house, opens the back door to the kitchen, and sees her brother eating cereal. He's reading a braille X-men comic of his favorite character, Cyclops. She goes to the sink and smiling as she washes her hands, she is so taken by the sight of both her hands under the water. Jordan says, "Why did you run out of the house like there was a fire or something?" Rebecca picks up a towel to dry her hands. She looks at Jordan and says, "Can you keep a secret?" Jordan replies, "Depends how much you're gonna pay me." He smiles. "Oh, I think you'll be paying me for this one, it's that good." She replies confidently. "Well, what are you waiting for then, spill the beans Becca." Jordan inquisitively retorts. She explains to Jordan what happened last night and what happened to her, she leaves out her dream though. His disbelief makes him spring out of his chair and grab on to his sister, feeling her fully functioning left arm. "No way!!!" he remarks. "I know right?" she exclaims. "Would you be willing, to take a chance to see again?" she asks. He blurts out, "Um yeah, duh!!" "Okay take my hand." She says still giddy, she reaches out her left arm to Jordan. When they get to the barn Jordan freezes and says, "This is not gonna hurt right?" "No, quite the opposite bro." she laughs. Rebecca takes her brother's hand and guides him to crouch down over the pulsing purple Orb and he says, "You better not be playing a joke on me." "No joke literally, you'll see." She says, and they both laugh a little at the pun. Rebecca then says, "Okay you ready?" He says, "Well I didn't walk all the way to the barn, for nothing. Let's do this… Leeroy Jenkins!!" "Okay, reach your hand out." She says. Jordan slowly does it. "Alright now down," she says guiding him a little. He touches the Orb and Rebecca sees him go through the same experience she did, and same fashion he falls back yelling out "Holy Crap, that felt amazing! Can I do it again?" "No, I don't think it works like that, I think it's a one-time thing." Rebecca answers. "Well that sucks." Jordan says followed by, 'So when will I be able to see?" "I don't know, everything changed for me, when I woke up." She says. "Strange, I am feeling pretty tired right now. Like really tired." He says. "Okay let's get you to your room then," Rebecca says. She helps up her brother and guides him out and closes the barn door. And same as Rebecca, Jordan just makes it to the bed, and then he's out. She puts a blanket over him and closes his bedroom door.

No sooner her doing that, she hears a knock at the front door. She peeks out from the hallway and can see the silhouette of her friend Hope through the stained glass on the front door. "Shit!" she says. Rebecca runs to her room and grabs one of her old slings that she'd wear whenever she'd go out to the store, to hide her deformity. She puts it on and covers up her left arm as best she can. Rebecca opens the door to a very slow-moving Hope, she's sipping from one of two coffees in her hands. "Here I brought you one," Hope says reaching it out to Rebecca. "Thanks," Rebecca replies. "Don't thank me yet I may drink yours to stay awake," Hope says as she plops down on the living room couch. "AAAARGH!!" Hope burst out in frustration, 'I hate my parents, and I can't wait to go away to college. I didn't get any sleep at all last night, they were arguing so loud, screaming and yelling, I wanted to call the cops on them. Then finally, when they passed out, I dozed off, and then BOOM!!! A loud something exploded, I think over my house. Dogs were barking, car alarms were going off, so this little lady got no sleep. How was your night?" Rebecca sits down next to Hope, looks down at her sling "Oh boring, watched T.V. then went to sleep." She says awkwardly. "You didn't hear that boom? I thought the whole state heard it, it's all over the news." Hope says. "Nope, didn't hear it," Rebecca says unconvincingly. Hope now suspicious, looks at her friend and says, "You know you're not a very good liar Becca." Just as Hope finishes saying that a small spider that was crawling on the ceiling, falls on the coffee table in front of the girls. They both instantly jump out of the couch screaming with hands flailing around. Hope stops and is staring at Rebecca who just realizes that her arm is out of the sling, and very visible. "How is your arm healed Becca?" Hope says confused. Rebecca now busted, closes her eyes, takes a deep breath, looks at her childhood friend, and says, "Let's go to the barn I have something to show you."

Rebecca quickly explains what happened to Hope on the walk to the barn, with Hope's green eyes wide open the whole time. Standing over the purple dome Hope asks, "Where do you think it came from? I can't believe you touched it, and I can't believe it healed your arm." "I don't know. I had a dream last night and I think they were in my dream." Rebecca says. "What do you mean they were in your dream? Who are they? What are they?" Hope exclaims. "I think they are called Remaks from a planet called Res but they were originally from a planet called Zan." Rebecca says. "What?!! They told you this in your dream?" Hope says hysterically. Rebecca then described her dream in detail to Hope, which took like an hour cause of how many times Hope would stop her asking questions in amazement. Rebecca even gestured to Hope to touch it, but she wanted nothing to do with the glowing magic purple Orb. After a while of various gasps from Hope, they walk out, close up the barn and go back to the house. They're in the kitchen still talking about it, when Hope asks "What are you going to tell your mom? Does your brother know?" Rebecca wincing says, "I had him touch it too." "Oh my god!" Hope shrieks. "Where is he?" she says. Rebecca says, "He's in bed in his room." Hope hurries down the hall with Rebecca slowly following. Hope peeks into Jordan's room and sees him asleep. They both walk into his room and stand looking at him… when he moves. Jordan is like a bear waking from a slumber, stretches, and yawns. Then slowly he opens his eyes, trying to focus, he sees his sister and says, "I can see you Becca". Both girls instantly start crying as they rush to lavish Jordan with hugs and kisses. Rebecca and Jordan, banter back and forth saying "I see you, I see you." laughing with tears of joy the whole time. Hope steps back and pulls out her phone, takes a quick Instagram pic of the brother and sister with big smiles, as both of them give a two-handed thumbs up. They were all full of excitement, little did they know that pic was about to make them famous.

chapter three

VIRAL

On that very morning three miles away from Rebecca's house in the Charleston household, things weren't as joyful. Beverly Charleston 18, who also recently graduated from the very same high school as Rebecca and Hope, was not having as good morning. Beverly who was always in a t-shirt and Jeans grew up in a broken home. Her older brother Bradley was killed six months ago due to gang violence, leaving her alone with their mother. Stella Charleston 38, was hurt in a work accident, which lead to her finding out she had hip dysplasia. The condition restricted her mobility to a walker, and she's been living off disability checks for two years. The house she lived in was cluttered and small, hardly room for two. There was never a father in the picture, from birth he was locked up, five years in, he was killed in his jail cell. Beverly's only male role model was her older brother, who was now dead at the age of 21. She hustled here and there to make it day by day. Her brother's street smarts, whom he passed down, shaped her self-sufficiency. She grew up closed off with a non-trust of others and never really having a close friend. Beverly had a lot of rage in her, she was mad she was poor, mad her mom was an invalid, mad her brother was gone, and mad cause she saw no way out. Which frustrated her the most because she graduated high school with a 3.67 grade point average. However, she couldn't leave and go into the military, or college like others, her mom needed her. She was stuck.

Beverly and Rebecca were not friends, even though they grew up together throughout school. Beverly was jealous of her and her ability to make friends despite her deformity. In 7th grade, she made fun of Rebecca by calling her twist, making a reference to her arm. A major shouting match ensued, between Rebecca's and Beverly's friends. Beverly's group wasn't as large but was a menacing click. Nothing ever happened, but from that day they each just kept to their own area. Mean looks would sometimes be shared, but no one on Beverley's side wanted to be known for getting in a fight with a disabled person. The street cred would not increase much. Rebecca would have never backed down from a fight and Beverly knew this. This went on till this day, but today would not be the typical day for either girl.

On this morning, Beverly was sent out to run an errand for her mother. A trip to the grocery store for eggs and milk, and then to the pharmacy for her pain prescription. And passing Rebecca's house, just so happened to be en route to Beverly's mom's pharmacy. Already finished with the grocery shopping she drove her mom's beat-up 1998 Pontiac Bonneville to the pharmacy. She glanced like always, at the Marshall House in passing and made her way to pick up her mom's medicine. At the pharmacy, they ran out of her mom's generic medication and only had the original brand name, which cost eight times more. Beverly yells at the pharmacist that her mom can't afford this, then storms out, after having to use the rest of her own money to pay for the prescription. While she's sitting in her car, she sees the Instagram post of Rebecca and her brother all happy in their pic. She is angry at the world and her life and there's no better person she sees to take out her vengeance on other than Rebecca.

Meanwhile, back at the Marshall house. The tears and hugs have calmed down, Rebecca and Jordan are talking about the particularly similar dream they had. Jordan asks, "So it took them like 1000 years to get here, moving that fast?" "Seems so." Rebecca replies. "So, they are just combined energy, how do they eat? Do they poop? Or sleep?" Jordan asks perplexed. "I don't know Jordan, it wasn't quite explained." Rebecca says laughing. Hope says, "I need a smoke to calm my nerves, let's go on the porch and continue this." They go and sit on the porch furniture which consists of a bench and two rocking chairs... the girls take the chairs. As they're talking, a car rolls up alongside and stops at the entry to the property. The passenger side window rolls down and a voice yells out "I see you got the twist out, you ready to finish this!" Hope exclaims, "Oh shit, that's that bitch Beverly!" Hope yells back, 'Bring it on Bitch!!" No sooner, Beverly is out of her car running up the grass/gravel driveway. Rebecca runs off her porch to confront her. The two meet up, and immediately start trading blows to the face and body. Rebecca is noticeably stronger, even though visibly she's outmatched. She's thin and only 5'6" to Beverly's stocky 5'10" frame. Beverly, already bleeding from her nose and lip is knocked to the ground, she gets up and gets knocked down again by another crushing blow. This time she picks up a wooden baseball bat laying on the ground. She stands up holding the bat at ready, the two girls' eyes glare as the hot sun beams down on them. Then Beverly delivers an overhead swing, Rebecca throws up her left arm to block the strike, and then there's a loud crack, SNAP! The bat splits in two, the top half goes flying 20 feet away... Beverly is shocked by what she sees and so is Rebecca. Rebecca stares at Beverly and says, "As Captain America said, I can do this all day..." Beverly drops the bat handle and runs back to her car, then speeds off, all while being heckled by Jordan and Hope. Hope who filmed the whole thing on her phone looks at Rebecca in awe, she has not a scratch on her. Jordan says, "Becca did the Orb make you stronger? It looked like you kicked her ass with no effort." Rebecca looks at Hope and Jordan and says, "I don't know, I felt like I was fighting in slow motion, I could see everything she was about to do like I was Neo. But how did she know my arm was healed?" Hope says innocently, "I posted the pic I took of you two to Instagram." Hope says panicky, "Oh my god what did I do?" she looks at the pic comments and it has gone viral. Rebecca runs inside the house to check her phone, and she has a bunch of text messages from every one of her friends, all asking about her arm. Rebecca screams out, "Hope, what did you do?!! Delete the post now!" Rebecca says. Hope replies hysterically, "Okay, I know I'm so sorry. We'll think of something. Let's say you had surgery." Rebecca replies, "Surgery!! We just graduated two days ago, Hope.

People aren't that stupid to think I could have had surgery and healed in two days." Hope replies, "I know, I know, what if we just said it was a joke and we photoshopped your arm?" Rebecca replies, "Um, I just kicked Beverly's ass, she's not gonna think her bruises and blood is photoshopped. I'm sure she ain't gonna say anything, but she knows the arm is healed and maybe a bit more than just healed. It's not every day you break a bat over one. Just don't reply to anyone, till we figure this out." Hope and Rebecca are squabbling back and forth in the living room, about excuses they can use to explain the phenomenon. When the calm quiet voice of Jordan says, "Why don't we just tell the truth? I mean this shouldn't just be for us, you know." The girls stop and look at him and he continues, 'Like, everyone should be able to get healed or fixed, we shouldn't keep it all to ourselves, that's not the kind of people we are." Rebecca takes a moment and sighs, "You're right little brother. Everyone in the world should be able to be healed from disease or disability." A moment of clarity settles over all of them. Hope chimes in, "Yea, and we could make it like a charity, donate to help Flint, and help yourself." Rebecca says, "Like $20 and bring a tent to sleep in. Hey, we have like 5 acres, for people to crash on." Hope says, "And we can get businesses from all over to pitch in, like port-a-potty and food trucks." Jordan says, "Ah um, you guys know mom doesn't know yet, she's gonna freak for sure about all of this." At this time, a vehicle rolls slowly onto the driveway and up to the house. Everyone jumps up to see who it is. It's Uncle Pete, in his lifted 2019 Dodge truck. Uncle Pete was Rebecca and Jordan's favorite uncle, he was tall, dark, and thin, with a shiny bald head. Rebecca would often say as a joke, he reminded her of Xerxes from the movie 300. Rebecca says, "Hurry up. Let's play a joke on him." They all run back to the couch and turn on the TV, they cover up Rebecca's arm and Jordan puts his shades on, Hope just sits in the middle of them on the couch. Uncle Pete walks in through the front door, a little tired from his drive from Lansing. He says in his happy way, "Hi kids, Maggie's not home yet huh?" No one answers him, as he makes his way through the house to the bathroom. The three are giggling and whispering when he comes out of the bathroom. He says, "What's the joke?" Rebecca says, "Well, Hope here says, that copper nugget on the coffee table wasn't real, and I kinda agree with her." This was in reference to a giant, one-pound copper nugget, Pete found while hiking through the Caledonia mine area, in northern Michigan when he was a teenager. He was immensely proud of his discovery, so much he deeply carved his full initials into it, to forever stake his claim. They all knew the story and knew it would get a rise out of Uncle Pete. And on cue, Uncle Pete picked up the nugget re-examining it, like he'd just discovered it for the first time again, and said, "Damn right its real, I found it two miles northwest, off a trail up there at Caledonia mine, under a large sycamore tree when I was no older than Jordan." Jordan stands up from the couch, dust his clothes off to build the theatrics, walks up to Uncle Pete, and lifts up his shades grabs the nugget from his uncle. He does a slight inspection and says, "Yep it's real." Then throws it to his sister, who catches it with her left hand. And she says, "Hmmm, you may be right." At this time Pete yells out, "You can see...You can catch???!!!" All while pointing at his niece and nephew, then he faints. Moments later, Pete who has been put on the couch by the kids, slowly comes to. He can hear as he's being shook back and forth, "Uncle wake up, come on, wake up!" shouting to him by Jordan and Rebecca. He opens his eyes in a daze and says, "What happen, did I faint?" "Yea, you fainted, here's some water." Rebecca says handing him a glass of water. "You okay?" "Yea I'm alright, what the hell happened to you guys, how'd your arm get fixed, and how is Jordan able to see? All the doctors said he'd be blind for life." Pete asks confused. "Well uncle, I'll explain it all, but I think you should remain on the couch for this." Rebecca comfortingly replies. Rebecca, Jordan, and Hope all unload their parts to what happened like a tsunami to Pete, who takes it all in as if he's watching an intense movie. After they all say their part, Pete asks, "Can I see it?" Being a geologist, you could understand his curiosity, a rock from outer space. How could he resist? As they walk to the barn, Uncle Pete's nice leather shoes are getting soaked from the soft wet soil under the grass, but he doesn't care, he's so excited to see this gift from the heavens. He's walking so fast the kids are almost having to run to keep up.

Once in the barn, they all form a circle around the purple pulse. The band of green grass has slightly grown bigger. It looks like the top of a purple man's balding head, with green hair growing around it.

The Orb's pulse seems a little bit brighter as if it's happy to see them, or that's what Rebecca felt, even though she didn't say anything. Pete says, "Why is there a grass ring growing around it?" Rebecca says, "I don't know, in the dream, I think for them, light provides life. So maybe whatever it touches, gets infected with life." "I wonder how deep it's embedded." Pete says as he stoops down to get a better look. He quickly jumps to his feet and says, "Don't move I'll be back." He runs to his truck grabs a leather satchel and comes back to the barn. He then uses scissors to cut the grass back from the Orb, being very careful, not to come into contact with it. He then blows the grass away and leans in with his magnifying glass. As he leans in, the group of teens does likewise. Pete says with disbelief, "It's flawless, I mean I can't tell about the rest that's buried, but from what I am looking at, the surface of this is without imperfections. Whatever this is, it's unlike anything I've ever seen before." No sooner he says that Pete reaches into his bag for his rock hammer he says, "Maybe I can get a chip of this, to take back to the lab to examine." As he says this Rebecca says cautiously, "No, I don't think you should do that uncle." Pete says, "It's okay, I collect rock samples all the time. I'm just gonna take a small chip." He raises the hammer up and very softly strikes the edge of the Orb…. On contact there is a deafening continuous gong, so loud the barn starts shaking almost to collapse. Everyone runs out of the barn covering their ears. The gong echoes as it carries throughout the area for miles. You can hear dogs barking in the distance, and car alarms going off. It finally subsides, after five seconds, the gang all have ringing in their ears. Rebecca walks up to her uncle and yells, "Don't you ever do that again, are you trying to kill us!?" In shock and apologetic, her uncle says, "I'm so sorry guys, you okay? Listen, I'm gonna take some pictures and go get someone who may be able to explain this, and where it's from, don't touch it again." He then runs back into the barn. Rebecca and Jordan look at each other shrugging their shoulders, and Jordan says, "I thought we already explained to him where it came from… grown-ups go figure." Pete then runs out of the barn, back to his truck yelling, "Remember kids don't touch it, I'll be back, tell your mom I'll see her tomorrow, I love you." "Okay, love you too uncle." Rebecca and Jordan mumbling say together. The kids close the barn and go back to the house. They are all standing around the kitchen, still rubbing their ears. "Well, at least we know never to hit the Orb," Hope says. They all look at each other and nod. Then Jordan says, "I'm starving" followed by, 'Holy crap I can see, I can make whatever I want. You know what? I am making dinner tonight! Hope, you want to join us for dinner?" Rebecca and Hope laugh. Hope excitedly says, "Hell yea, what ya making?" Jordan confused, "I don't know… I've never cooked before." He looks at his sister for a lifeline, Rebecca graciously says, "It's alright bro, let's make dinner together, I'll be your sous chef." Jordan exclaims, "Alright let's do this, mom's gonna flip, it's going to be delicious! I see you, sis." Rebecca says "I see you, bro."

When Maggie gets home about an hour later, she walks in through the front door and into a robust aroma of fried chicken and mashed potatoes that fills the house. Suspiciously, Hope is sitting on the couch to greet her with a glass of Merlot wine, and her bedroom slippers set aside, waiting. Hope says, "Hi Miss Marshall, I need you to please sit down, we have a surprise for you." Hope pats the couch, 'Rest yourself right here on the couch and let me trade your shoes out." Hope gets up off the couch, as she guides Maggie to sit. Warily Maggie says, "What are you kids up to? What did you break?" "Oh, quite the contrary, it's been an amazing day. Miss Marshall nothing is broken, but I'll leave the rest to your kids to explain." Hope replies. Hope puts two chairs facing the couch then calls out, "Okay, I think she's ready." Rebecca guided Jordan to walk slowly out of the kitchen door, wearing the sling and sunglasses like before, and sit in the chairs facing their beloved mother. Hope says, "I'm gonna go get some water, just in case." Rebecca and Jordan proceed to tell and show their mom what happened to them. There is a series of loud, Oh My Gods!! And joyful tears and laughter. This goes on, for a while till when night has fallen. The kids take their mom to the barn where she sees the healing Orb. It's very dark, except for the Orb's bright pulse, which illuminates the barn like a nightclub. The light is very soothing, and they watch it for a moment until the silence is broken by Jordan's appeal, "Okay can we go eat now, please!" They all nod and laugh in agreement, Maggie says as they walk back to the house, "So can I expect to come home to dinner every night now?" Jordan replies, "You know what mom you just might, I love cooking, I mean I think

I'm a natural." Rebecca says awkwardly, "Mom I have to admit, he's not bad. Maybe not seeing made his taste buds better, but the kid knows his way around spices." Maggie replies laughing, "Well today has just become better than Christmas." Everyone gets back to the house, and the kids tell their mom the additional stories of the day, including Beverly and Pete. Which Maggie has mixed feelings about it, she does not approve of Rebecca fighting but did understand, it was to protect herself. When it came to her brother Pete, she recalled hearing the gong, and she was ten miles away. The four keep talking over dinner, and Jordan revels in all the compliments he's receiving. Hope decides to spend the night so they can work on the social media problem, and heal their world endeavor.

chapter four

REMAKS AND THE RETAKS

The night carries on brainstorming creative ideas about healing people and exaggerated revenues to help the city of Flint. As it got late, one by one everyone went to bed. Like always, Hope slept in Rebecca's bed which was a king-size, big enough for them both. Rebecca was last to drift off to sleep and like the night before, her dream took her on a mental escapade.

Again she awakens in her dream, she's back in the big dark room. A cursor flickers on and becomes a hologram of a planet. Rebecca stands, looking down upon the foreign world and she hears the unison voices say, "Zan, our first home." She is then zoomed onto the planet, to what looks like the early years of the Remak's history. They look the same as they did in early Res, they still dressed, quite simple. The equipment though does not look as advanced as before. Rebecca is watching an exploration being carried out by six Remaks. They are walking through a very dense forest. The trees are massive, with trunks 20ft wide and 200ft high. They have black bark and orange-colored leaves. The branches and red vines wrapped around the trees are aware of the foreign beings and reach out to touch the Remaks. Like they were touching them out of curiosity, inspecting the new visitors in their midst. Rebecca hears the familiar voices again say "Zalar." She turned around looking for the voices and yelled, "Come out here and explain this, stop whispering words to me!" Then out of the darkness, a glowing purple figure emerges. Taller than Rebecca by a foot, but she's not afraid, she feels that same warm comfort feeling from the barn. The unison voices say "Zalar is our word for forest." She points and says excitedly, "You're from the Orb." The voices say, "We are." Rebecca asks, "How do you know our language?" They reply, "We analyzed your radio broadcast on our journey to you, we also studied your cultures, religions, and customs, they were all very interesting. Your country's wars and the constant fight for power is one of the reasons we sought you out." Rebecca replies confused, "I don't understand, you want us to keep fighting?" The voices say, "No, we want you to see there's a better way than fighting and killing. Resorting to such means, only when necessary. On our way here, we have encountered many lifeforms, but none as interesting as you. Your species has the most potential in five galaxies." The glowing figure is now right in front of Rebecca. It doesn't have distinct features more like a tall purple human-like silhouette. She's looking up at the being, dumbfounded, it points to the forest hologram behind her. Rebecca turns around and the voices say, "Let us show you some more of our history, we have so much to share with you."

The hologram goes in motion, she sees the exploration team make their way to a clearing at the edge of the forest. It looks like a primitive village colony of only about five hundred beings. There are many half-clothed bodies busy working. Farming the land by hand with rocks and pieces of tree bark. Some are sowing and some dig up potato-like crops from the ground. They live in big communal soil mounds covered by orange grass. It's hard to tell which is male or female from what Rebecca sees, their smaller young ones running about playing. They were or what looked like the Retaks. Rebecca asks, "They're Retaks?" The voices say, "Yes this is where we discovered them, early into our history. The six explorers were on an expedition to find a mineral called Vemil, which we refine for energy. They stumbled upon their colony. At first, the colonist was skeptical of interaction, until one of the explorers took out of his backpack an expandable spade-like shovel. He demonstrated using it to dig and plant in the soil. The Retaks were so impressed with the new tool, the explorer handed it to one of them. This, however, infuriated another Retak who wanted it. They fight it out right there to the death, with the victor being the original possessor, killing the challenging Retak with the said shovel." Rebecca is watching in amazement as this is all portrayed visually before her eyes as if she is there. She gasps, "Oh my god!" as she watches the shovel penetrate the neck of the victim. The Remaks apologize, "We are sorry to show you such violence." Rebecca replies, "It's okay, just wasn't expecting that. You can keep going." The Remaks nod and continue, "After seeing this display of hostility, the explorers grew genuinely concerned that they may be next. But surprisingly, no aggression is shown towards the Remaks. The explorers roamed around the colony freely, except for a few curious grunts and growls here and there. We Remaks you see, are not violent, and defending ourselves has always been a dilemma for us. We are creators and researchers, incapable of causing harm, even to each other. The Retaks at the time were more of a primitive mindset, and we thought we could change that. The head Remak explorer named Mas, who was the most experienced, asked the Retaks in gestures to come with them back to the Remaks world. The head of the Retaks, Camba said no to the entire village leaving but did allow six from the colony to leave, four males and two females. All the volunteers were young adults except one, an older male, sent as a protector/overseer and would report back if things ever went awry."

The visual landscape magically changes around Rebecca, she sees a colony full of hundreds of giant domes all connected with tubes that travel for miles. Like an interconnecting honeycomb web. She then sees the Retaks in a classroom setting being shown different skills and teachings. The voices say, "We brought the Retaks to a learning area, and taught them what we knew, the young ones learned slowly but steadily. The older male was apprehensive at first, but he came around eventually when we introduced him to our version of cars. Which are like your earth cars, except they hovered and were controlled mentally. He liked the very fast ones and enjoyed driving them over the land and ocean. Years went by, and the Retakes evolved with their new understanding. They would periodically go back to their colony and show them new tools and what they had learned. Then curious, more would leave the colony to seek this new world of knowledge."

"A couple of centuries passed and the Retaks grew to One hundred thousand beings. We learned about defense and created weaponry from the ideas of the Retaks, who were great hunters and fighters. And the Retaks along with modern living, learned science, and exploration of the stars from us, something we'd later regret. The Retaks took what they had learned, and migrated to isolated areas where it was just them and no Remaks, we thought it was for the sense of community. The Retaks did not own, or have anything other than what we gave them, so they felt like pets, and missed their free nomad ways. Only a few Retaks lived amongst us, mainly those banished by the head Retak, for crimes against the tribe. Like mating with a Remak or stealing from a fellow Retak. The Retaks even though they learned had limited capacity, they could only do what they were shown, and creativeness was still the gift of the Remaks. They had a difficult time comprehending, "The out of the box thinking." as you from earth would say. The Retaks had a comfortable life, existing in leisure, and could live an easy life, till death, if they chose to. We concluded this was too easy for them. They did not own a claim to anything, and many of them felt they wanted more. What was mostly true is, we had suppressed their hunting and aggressive proclivity so long, and it was just a matter of time before they erupted.

Around this time, a young Retak named Jak, who was ambitious and power-hungry, conspired to overthrow us and rule everyone. He said to his inner circle, "We are bigger and stronger we can rule the Remaks and have them make everything we want." So, the Retaks let their inner instinct take over. They planned a coup, which started with Jak killing the head Retak and assuming leader for the tribe. Their plan took ten years to carry through. After they learned all they could. They would kill all but a few thousand of us and then enslave us. And as we are passive species, it took all but a week to carry out once they started their plan. In the end, there were only about a thousand Remaks left, they had all but wiped us out of existence. They helped us prepare for an extraterrestrial threat from the stars, with blaster cannons and in Orbit beam cannons. Unbeknownst to us, we had crafted our demise, to forever imprison us on our own planet. The enslavement went on for three hundred years, we only mate every five years, so we waited till our numbers were up, for a better chance of some surviving. After we secretly found a planet we could inhabit, we developed a plan of escape. Rebecca interrupts confused, "What you guys never fight, why didn't you defend yourselves? Why didn't you kill them all?" The voices say, "We just have never been like that, we are peaceful and non-confrontational, hence the reason we are so curious about it. When one of us thinks differently we analyze research, and create. It has produced various idea paths, which have enhanced our development. We welcome, all thoughts and ideas. Your society has been fighting and killing every day for centuries. What have you really gained from it? You could be so much more. We relish the differences in each other and try to combine as one." Rebecca responds, "Yea I guess you're right, we could be better. But there are a lot of mean people in the world, greedy and spiteful, that are only out for themselves. I don't think that'll ever change." The unison voices reply, "You will change that." Rebecca's eyes widen and she says excitedly, "What?!! Me, no not me I'm a kid, I don't want that kind of responsibility. Is that why you're talking to me? No. Please pick someone else!! No No No No!" Rebecca awakens and sits up in bed in a panic heart racing and breathing heavily. She says to herself "Oh my god what did I get myself into." She quietly gets out of bed, trying not to wake Hope, and goes to the kitchen. She pours herself a glass of cold milk from the fridge. As she drinks it her eyes are glued, to the dark silhouette of the barn, she is thinking about its glowing occupant. It's 2:35 am, Rebecca opens the back door and puts on some rubber boots that her mom leaves there. It's a nice cool night, she can hear the crickets chirping as she walks through the wet grass. She wants answers and she is going to get them, I didn't sign up for this shit, she thinks. She closes the barn door behind her and goes and sits Indian-style next to the Orb. She asks, "What the hell is going on? You want me to change the world? Is that why you healed my arm. If that's the case take it back now. What you're asking is impossible." She waits for a response and the Orb just keeps pulsing. Rebecca is getting frustrated and yells, "Answer me you purple piece of shit!" as she says this, she slams the Orb with both hands. She contacts the Orb, she sees a flash before her eyes and she's knocked out, her body drops lifeless onto the hay.

Rebecca awakens in the dream and hears the voices say, "We are sorry Rebecca, but this is what you were destined to do. You are not alone, we are always here for you to answer anything you ask but can only communicate with you when you are in a dream state. You are very strong Rebecca and a gift to the world, we are honored to have picked you." Rebecca replies "What the hell. So you picked me, how!?" The voices reply, "We will get to that, let us finish with our history so you understand us being here." Rebecca replies, "Okay, but I still don't want to be your Neo." The voices continue, "Our numbers were around three thousand families spread out around our planet. In the three hundred years that passed, our elders had developed a secret way of communicating through our dreams. They devised a plan and under the ground of each family living dome, we built small shuttles, big enough for each family. They disguised portal jumpers as Orbiting cannons, programmed to space jump the shuttles to a star system light- years away to an inhabitable planet. The plan did not work, as they all took off the Retaks shot them out of sky and space. All but one ship made it through the portals. They arrived at a planet they named Res, a planet like their planet Zan but untouched, new, and safe. The planet was inhabited with nothing threatening to the Remaks survival, and for 1500yrs our beings evolved so much, we became able to travel out of our physical bodies using light as our mode of transport." Rebecca chimes in, "That's so cool." The voices say, "It's was a nice way to get around Zan, on the white sun rays we would ride like you surf waves. You may tell, you are listening to more than one of us, but yet all of us at the same time. We think and act collectively presently, in the Orb. There are eight of us, we were each born to separate families but studied and worked on Zan in a remote underground dome together. We were young Remaks four females Sendu, Moo, Wicka, and Beato, and four males Clak, Gatree, Aredez and Tooloo. We were always together living and working for the betterment of Remaks everywhere. Then one day, it happened all at once, while we were working on a travel Orb. Thousands of Retaks dropped down from the skies in vessels and started destroying and killing all that they saw. They use guns that disintegrated every living thing they shot, not even escaping our bodies could save us. The guns shot antimatter bullets that absorbed everything, even light. They invaded quickly and everywhere at once. Domes and tunnels were being destroyed separating families from getting to each other, they killed without malice young and old. We came up outside, from our underground lab. We watched explosions in the distance, as all our family Remaks perished, a sadness grew amongst us to know that. This was a tragic day, that forever bound us together. Our lead Sendu and Tooloo made the decision, for us to leave, save our species in the new creation we had developed. We had no time and only seconds to react for the Retaks would soon be there. We opened our dome top, luckily the white sun shone, breaking through the black smoke and ashes of destruction. We each discarded our bodies of birth and once again our species ran into a shuttle, to escape from the Retaks. Our spacecraft traveled using the sun's beams of light, like a zipline. We found the strongest ray, locked on to it, and in seconds we were shot into space. We zipped past the giant mothership the Retaks had created and would come to find out not all the Remaks had been killed on Zan." Rebecca sees a monstrous black icosahedron-shaped ship, hovering over the planet Res. The voices continue, "They used Remaks to create a spaceship, and eventually, after searching the universe, they found us, they found Res. It was all done to hunt down the escaped descendants from Zan. We became the greatest prey the Retaks had ever encountered, it was all a challenge to them, to erase us from existence. We were the last of our kind, trapped in a purple teardrop, whipping through space on light waves, looking for a new home. Using our knowledge of portals, we created light portals that could allow us to travel to different galaxies via light bridges." Rebecca sees the Orb project a beam, like a car headlight, it's a telescoping green ring that cuts a circle into space, a doorway. Once the ship entered, it was in an entirely different solar system. The vessel enters and exits repeatedly, in and out of multiple galaxies. The voices continue, "We searched for 800yrs looking for the right planet... then faintly, we picked up on some strange frequencies. Curious, we guided ourselves towards the source. As the frequencies got stronger, another 100yrs went by and could see the source, your planet. We learned your languages, theories, and customs from the radio and television transmissions. Once we arrived at your Earth, we watched you all for a few years more. Your daily exchanges with each other, are quite peculiar. We see all life, in auras of light. To us, you all look like variations of colored light, moving through your daily lives. Each of your interactions briefly, trades a little of your color with one another. Then moments later you all go back to your natural color. Everyone has a color, some dark some bright, each one of you, has one individual color, all except you Rebecca. You are all the colors and your white light shines bright. Your interaction light trail resonates longer than anyone else, you are memorable... That's why we came to you. We chose you because you are the light."

Everything goes black.

chapter five

THE LIGHT

Rebecca awakens, to her brother and Hope looking down at her curled up on the hay, next to the Orb. Hope's wearing one of Rebecca's Marvel Ironman t-shirts. Hope says jokingly, "I didn't think I took up that much of the bed." Rebecca replies, "HaHa funny, I came out here to get some answers." She gets up covered in straw, it's stuck to her hair, face, and clothes. Hope says, "And?" Rebecca replies as she beats off the straw, "Oh I got answers, I got a whole history lesson, you won't believe the craziness I'm about to tell you." She looks at her brother, "Jordan, did you dream of them last night?" Jordan replies, "Not really, I dreamt I could really see far away stuff, like miles away, weird." He shakes his head. Rebecca leads them out of the barn, "Okay, I need a shower to get all this hay off me, Jordan start on breakfast since you're a chef now. Hope you look nice in my shirt, but you're not keeping it." Rebecca says commandingly as they walk back to the house. It's a beautiful Sunday morning, the sun is radiating through the coolness of the morning air. Rebecca closes her eyes and raises her face to catch the sun's rays and she smiles.

While the girls ate a standard breakfast Jordan made, of bacon and eggs. Chef Jordan YouTubed, how to make a quiche. Rebecca explained to Jordan and Hope, what she experienced the night before. In the middle of her explanation, Maggie woke up. It was her day off and she normally slept in, but all the chatter coming from the kitchen woke her up. Maggie walks into the kitchen and says, "Do you all know it's my Sunday, why are you three making such noise this early? And what's that interesting smell, WooWee… is that quiche?" Jordan replies, "Yes mom sure is." "Well look at my chef son, yesterday you couldn't find the pantry, today you're making quiche. That Orb shoulda dropped down here sooner." Maggie makes her a plate and sits at the table and says, "So what are you all rumbling about?" Rebecca replies, "Mom, this was no mistake, the Orb said it chose me." Maggie says, "Chose you? Like it knew where to find you here on earth, and just crashed into our barn?" Rebecca replies, "Yes, basically. They can see us, I mean they've been looking at us for a while. We look like colored light to them and I'm like all the colors in one. They said they chose me because I am the light and I'm gonna change the world." Maggie stops eating, looks at her daughter, and says, "Baby, there's no doubt you are special, you were from birth and I could see that from here. If these Remaks can see that from space. Well then my daughter, fulfill your destiny." Everyone stops as Maggie continues with eating. Rebecca says, "Mom did you touch the Orb?" Maggie says, "You damn right I did. When you all were in the room last night planning your whatever. I wasn't gonna let what infected my children, go without me knowing what it was. I raised you, I need to know all about your wellbeing." She smiles. Rebecca questions, "Did they talk to you?" Maggie replies "They sure did. They explained your importance and that I need not worry, and I believe them. This quiche is amazing Jordan!" Maggie looks at her son and smiles as she chomps down on her last bite. She gets up, gets a glass of water, and heads back to her room while saying, "I'm going back to bed you kids keep it down and don't leave this house without telling me." She hums a song as she walks away, they heard her bedroom door shut and they all look at each other in amazement. Their mom was in quite a pleasant mood, which was unusual if someone woke her on Sunday morning. Jordan blurts out, "That Orb is the most magical thing ever!" Then all three laugh. Rebecca says, "Okay let's do a trial run, it's Sunday let's go to my Uncle Ed's church and pick out a person that needs help and bring them here." Jordan says, "That's an awesome idea, we can get someone who's blind." Hope follows with, "How about someone in a wheelchair?" Rebecca raises her hands,

"Okay ease up, let's go see first, okay?" they all nod their heads and smile.

Shortly thereafter, the gang's all dressed and ready to head out to the church. Rebecca sticks her head into her mom's room and says, "Mom we are going walk to Uncle Ed's." she replies, "Okay, tell my brother don't forget to order the flowers for mummy's and daddy's grave, the 10th is right around the corner." Rebecca replies, "Okay Mom, will do." George and Mary were buried on July 10th 1988, in the church cemetery Ed currently ministers at. Everyone in the family loved that because it was like Mary and George were always close by. Rebecca walked into the living room, to find Jordan and Hope standing there waiting and ready like soldiers before a mission. Rebecca says, "Like Elliot Ness said, alright now, let's go do some good." They all put a hand in and do a team shake. Rebecca says to Hope "Okay I'm ready to post a pic." Hope says "Yaaay!" Hope puts her phone held high. The three group up. Rebecca does the hand's heart sign, Jordan does a thumbs up, leaning to the side and Hope smiles her classic smile in between them. After the pic, Jordan looks at Hope and says, "You're really pretty." Hope face instantly turns as red as her hair, she tries to recover, saying all sassy, "Well now, I know your eyes are working, cause, you can see the truth!" she snaps her fingers and says, "Let's go!"

Its 9:45 am, they walk out of the house into a sunny day, the smell of summer is in the air. As they are about to get to the main road, they see a familiar Bonneville pull up and stop just short of them. It's hard for Rebecca to make out the two bodies in the car, due to the dark tinted windows. Jordan says, "It's that girl Beverly again and some older lady is with her." Rebecca looks at Jordan then at the car and yells, "You want some more, come on get out!" The driver's car door squeaks open and Beverly gets out. Her face bruised and swollen she walks towards them, slowly and meekly. Rebecca stands in front of the other two, rears her body, and fist up for another beating. Beverly puts both her hands up and says, "I'm not here for that. I'm here to apologize, please hear me out." Rebecca hesitant… says cautiously, "Okay, say what you want to say then go." Beverly looks back at the car then to Rebecca and says, "My mother saw me yesterday after our fight and asked me who did it. I didn't want to tell her at first, then

I did, she was so disappointed in me. Not because we fought, but why... I've hated you for so long with your nice family and friends and life. I hated that you, even with a deformed arm, could be so loved and happy. Whereas, I suffered and lost always while growing up. I know it had nothing to do with you, it's because I hated myself and my life. Yesterday, I went to get my mother's prescription, it used up all the money I had. I felt my life options were hopeless and the world was against me. Then seeing the Instagram post of you happy and healed, I flipped." Rebecca glares at Hope wide-eyed. Beverly continues, "I blamed you for all I was going through and took it out on you...and lost again. I'm sorry Rebecca for everything, I don't expect you to forgive me, and I just wanted you to know." Beverly has tears rolling down her cheeks, she looks down on the ground and says, "I just wish could go back and be friends with you all these years. I have to take my mom to the hospital now, she's not doing too well. By the way, your arm healed nice, now you're perfect...but then you always were." Beverly turns and starts walking back to the car. Rebecca turns around looking at Jordan and Hope with big eyes, Jordan's head nods, and shoulder shrugs and Hope winces. Rebecca pauses then calls out, "What's wrong with your mom?"

chapter six

IT BEGINS

Beverly and her mother Stella are invited into the house to talk, where the two girls finally made peace. Jordan served them some warm leftover quiche, which easily won them over. Maggie woke up about noon and joined everyone after she showered. It was all subtle pleasantries, till Stella asked the question, "Rebecca if you don't mind me asking. How did your arm heal?" Rebecca looks at Stella sitting at the kitchen table, and with a matter of fact, look says, "What if I told you some aliens from a distant world, traveled billions of miles through space, crash-landed into our barn, I touched their spaceship, then I woke up next day, all healed. Would you believe me?" Stella and Beverly look at each other, then back and forth at Rebecca then burst out laughing. They then look around and see no one else is laughing with them, but instead smiling and nodding. Beverly says, "Is that why you can see?" as she looks at Jordan. Jordan says, "Yep!" then Maggie chimes in, "And that's why my sciatica is gone, not to mention the touch is quite pleasant." She says smiling. Beverly looks at Hope and she says, "Oh no, not me I haven't touched it,' she says proudly, 'I'm still a virgin." Maggie bursts out in laughter looking at Stella, "She has no idea what she's missing out on, hopefully, you'll understand soon." Just at this time, a truck drives up the driveway. Maggie calls out, "Pete's here." As she opens the front door for him, he kisses her on the cheek as he walks by, and introduces, "This is

Professor Edward Lambkin" as the gentleman follows him into the house. The man is in his 50's Caucasian, bald with glasses. "Professor Lambkin is our head astrophysicist at Michigan State. He wanted to see the Orb. It's still in the barn, right?" Pete asks. Both gentlemen and Maggie make their way to the kitchen, where there's a brief silence that's interrupted by Rebecca saying in Scottish, "Well, we didn't get dressed up for nothing. Let's stop wasting time and head to the barn."

All eight stand in a circle on the newly grown grass, looking down at the purple pulse. The grass has grown to a patch circling the Orb, at least ten feet wide. Professor Lambkin asks, "Did this grass grow because of that?" he points to the Orb looking at Rebecca. She says nodding, "Yep." He then asks, "Have they communicated with you?" She says, "Yep." "Are they talking to you now?" he asks. "No, I can only talk to them in my dreams." He asks, "What do they want, where did they come from?" "Why don't you touch it and you can ask them yourself," she replies. He looks at her like a child at his first day in school, excited and scared. He bends down and Rebecca says smiling, "Where no man has gone before." He looks at her, lets out a chuckle, then touches the Orb. After the experience, the Professor falls back onto the fresh grass. Elated he exclaims, "Oh my god that was the most amazing feeling I've ever felt. I'm tingling!" Maggie says laughing, "Okay Professor come with me back to the house, I know what's next, and lemme get the guest room ready for you." With a big grin still on his face, he fixes his glasses on his face and is led out of the barn by Maggie. Rebecca looks at Stella and says, "You want to get your groove back?" Stella looks at Beverly and says, "I'm scared baby will you do it with me?" Beverly replies, "Yes mama I'll do it with you." Stella because of her disability needs help. Rebecca and Beverly get on each side of her, and help her down to her knees, while Jordan takes the walker away from in front of her. Beverly and Stella are now holding hands a tear falls from Stella's cheek onto the Orb and on the impact it splashes off the Orb and turns pink as it drops into the grass. Both women look at each other and grin in surprise. Then Beverly says softly, "Come on mom." They both reach out and touch the Orb. Moments later, the laughter and giddiness from the two women fill the barn. Jordan and Rebecca help Stella to her feet and Jordan and Hope escort the two back to the house. Rebecca looks at her uncle and says, "We need to tell Uncle Ed." Pete says, "Let me do it, I'll go today after he's done with church and pick him up, that'll give me time to talk to him. I don't think he's gonna be as excited about this as we are." Rebecca asks, "Are you going to touch it?" Pete replies, "Maybe, lemme talk to my brother first, I don't want him to feel like we left him out of this." Rebecca nods and smiles and says, "I love you, Uncle Pete." "I love you too kiddo, now hi-five me with that new arm of yours." She gives him the highest high five with her left hand and shouts out, "That's the first time I've ever done that, and this is awesome!" Laughing they close up the barn and head back to the house.

It was 4:30 pm now Professor Lambkin, Stella and Beverly had been asleep for about four hours. Uncle Pete left at 3pm to go get his brother, on his way he gave Hope a ride home. Maggie went to the store, to pick up some vegetables for a dinner salad. Chef Jordan was making Jambalaya, from a recipe he saw online. He figured, their guest would be staying for dinner and would be mighty hungry when they woke up. Rebecca was sitting at the kitchen table texting her friends, trying to explain what happened to her, without freaking any of them out. It wasn't going so well. They were all asking the same questions as, "Why did she do it, does she feel different, what do they look like, etc." And she was having to repeat her answers to them. She was getting a little frustrated. But she knew it was all out of concern for her, so she answered each one as nicely as she could.

The first of the sleeping beauties to wake up was Beverly, she was asleep in the guest bedroom with her mom. She walks into the kitchen and all her bruises were healed, she looks like she's been rejuvenated. She quietly sits down at the table and just looks at Rebecca, who is just looking back at her also. She then blurts out, "That was amazing! The Remaks are so awesome, I feel different like I'm stronger or something." Rebecca says, "Well maybe, you saw what my arm did to the bat." "Holy Shit do you think I can do that too?" Rebecca replies, "I don't know maybe, do you want me to hit you with a bat or something?" Jordan stops stirring the pot on the stove and turns around, curious as to what her answer will be. Beverly says, "No!" she pauses and then ecstatically says, "Yes!" Rebecca laughs, "You sure?

Okay!" The girls get up and go out the backdoor. Jordan quickly turns down the heat on the pot and runs out of the kitchen saying, "Oh, I gotta see this!" Once in the backyard, Rebecca says, "You sure about this? You remember last time we did this, what happened." Beverly replies, "I know, I know but I think this time will be different." The two girls are standing facing each other a few feet apart. Rebecca says, "Okay let's go slow, how about I hit you with something small first before we go to swing away Merrill." Beverly puzzled by her reference asks, "What?" Rebecca replies, "It's a line from the movie Signs, I'm a bit of a movie nerd." Beverly replies with a chuckle, "Okay whatever." Rebecca gets a wooden handle rake, stands in front of Beverly, smiles, and says, "Alright where do you want it?" Beverly takes a deep breath and says, "Just go." Rebecca swings the rake and Beverly blocks it with her forearm. The rake handle breaks in two, one half flies 15 feet away. Beverly says, "I didn't feel a thing. Do another one!" Rebecca says, "Alright super girl." Rebecca goes and gets a shovel and a hoe from the barn shed. Blow after blow, she blocks, and they break, with no injury to Beverly. Finally, Rebecca says, "Ok Jordan, go get my aluminum bat." Jordan looks at Rebecca, then Beverly, she nods and says, "You heard her go get it." A minute later, Jordan runs back with the shiny silver bat and hands it over to his sister, while saying, "You know mom's gonna kill you for breaking all her farm tools." He then runs back to look from a safe distance. The girls look at each other and then the broken tools, Rebecca shoulder shrugs and say, "It was done in the name of science, right?" Beverly replies, "Bad ass science!" They laugh. Rebecca says, "You ready? This is a swing away Merrill." Beverly replies, "Hit me with your best shot." Rebecca rears up, swings and they hear the bat ring out like a home run hit. Beverly looks at Rebecca and says, "Was that your best shot? You hit like a girl." She then starts laughing and so does Rebecca, Jordan is stunned. Beverly says, "More." Rebecca swings, again and again, each block Beverly is unscathed. Just as the swing-a-thing is going on Maggie drives in and sees what's happening in the distance, she parks and gets out of the car yelling, "What the hell are you kids fighting about!" The girls yell back, "We are doing a science project!" Maggie walks up to them, as Jordan runs to the house. Maggie sees all the broken tools on the ground and yells, "Are

49

you girls out of your Damn mind! You broke all my tools, I hope you know you're buying every single one of these things back and not with any allowance cause you been cut off. Now get to the car and bring them groceries in the house. Then come out here and clean up this mess." The girls look at each other and smile and say together, "Yes Mom, sorry." They then look at the bat, it is dented all over. The girls walk to the car and Beverly whispers to Rebecca, "This is not over, I wanna see what else I can do." Rebecca winks at Beverly and smiles.

After the girls cleaned up the mess, everyone gathers in the usual spot, the kitchen. Sitting around the table, they listen to Beverly tell her dream, the same one they are all too familiar with. As she is telling her story, a bald man pops his head out of the kitchen door and says, "Hello everyone." He is greeted with, "Hello Professor Lambkin, how was your slumber?" asks Maggie. He replies "It was amazing. Did you all have the dream I had?" Rebecca says, "With the panda elephant and Remaks and Retaks. Yep, we all had that. It's like an intro film to the Remaks and how they came to be." The professor replies, "Yes, yes, and then an amazing thing happened, when I woke, I could see without my glasses. It's incredible!" Maggie says, "I kinda liked you with glasses." All the kids look at each other and gasp out. Maggie comes back with, "Yea, well deal with it, your momma has been reborn!" Rebecca says, "Professor, before the Orb, my left arm was deformed." Jordan jumps in with, "And I was 100 percent blind before the Orb." "And I had bad sciatica." Maggie says smiling, "Now I can bend and move in all types of positions." As she winks at the professor. Rebecca screams out "Mom!!" Maggie says, "Oh hush, I'm just messing around with the man. Dinner is almost ready so help me make the salad."

Its 7:15 pm, the unique yet familiar rumble of Uncle Pete's truck pulls up the driveway. The truck shuts off and two doors slam shut. Shortly after a tall, thin good looking black man with Fedora hat on, walks through the kitchen door. He removes the hat and greets everyone, "Good evening to you all." Maggie goes to her big brother and gives him a hug and kiss. Then Rebecca and Jordan walk up to him. He smells of Brut cologne. He gently grabs Rebecca's left arm and looks it over, smiles kisses her on her forehead, and says,

"Hallelujah!" Then he puts both hands on Jordan's face, looks him in the eyes, and says, "Praise God." He then sits down and says, "Smells wonderful in here what's for dinner?" Maggie replies, "Your nephew is quite the cook, he made Jambalaya." Uncle Ed says, "Well, what are we waiting for, let's eat."

Maggie puts the leaf on the table, to expand it to fit all the guests. There are not enough chairs, so Rebecca and Jordan take two folding chairs to fill the gap. As they all sit around the table eating the wonderful food, they share nods of approval and gratitude. Jordan feels like a renowned world chef and is relished to watch people enjoy a skill, he never knew he had. Rebecca says to Ed "So Uncle Ed did Uncle Pete tell you everything." Uncle Ed who is just about done eating finishes his plate puts down his utensils takes a sip of water, and says, "I was waiting till after dinner to address that, but I guess this is as good a time as any." Ed clasps his hands together on the table and says, "Today, coincidently I gave my sermon on false gods and prophets and believing in symbolic things and satanic rituals. I told my congregation that miracles only come from the divine, one true God Jesus Christ. I prayed with them and solidified their faith in our lord. We sang and rejoiced in his name. There were not many parishioners, but it was enough to know that the few that were there, were there because of faith in our savior. This gave me solace. Then my brother comes over and tells me an object traveled here from out of space, landed on our family property then healed my niece and nephew with just a touch. Ain't that a bitch... I know I cannot promise such feats of healing through my ministry, even though I believe it's possible. In a split second, I saw the future of my life's work flash before my eyes. No longer will people seek out the bible's teachings they will go to this easy new, foreign, and impetuous divinity. So be it, but I will not close my doors, I will stay the course. I will forever have a place where all can come pray to the one true savior." Just as Ed finishes his speech there's a loud shriek from the guest bedroom. Everyone runs to see what the disturbance is. They open the door to find Stella jumping around dancing and laughing. She exclaims, "I'm healed, I'm healed look at me!" Beverly is in shock to see her mom moving the way she is. She runs to her mother and they hug, Beverly crying, looks her mom up and down, and asks, "You're better mom?" she smiles and responds, "I'm all better baby." Beverly goes to Rebecca grabs her hands and says, "They told me in my dream, I have to protect you, and I swear to you right here right now, no harm will ever come to you as long as I live." Beverly hugs Rebecca and then goes to her mother and says, "Mom you hungry? There's delicious jambalaya." They head out to the kitchen Ed has seen enough he says, "Pete it's 9 o'clock I'm ready, take me back home, Maggie thanks for having me, kids love you. Jordan's dinner was out of this world. To everyone else nice meet you all." Maggie is walking with Ed out the front door when they see out of the darkness, three people walking up the driveway. As they approach, Maggie sees it's a teenage boy with his mother, and in between them little boy is wearing a beanie being hand led. The teenage boy says to Maggie, "Hello Ms. Marshall I'm a classmate of your daughter Rebecca, my name is Quintin Williams this is my mother Sue, and this my little brother Bobby. We heard how Rebecca is now healed and was hoping maybe, you can help my brother he has a tumor in his brain and it's in stage three. Please help us." Jordan and Rebecca are standing on the front porch looking at the three plead for help, Ed leans into Maggie, gives her a kiss on the cheek, and whispers, "And so, it begins." He then gets in the truck and Pete and he slowly drive out. Maggie looks on as they leave, she feels strange as if her big brother is disappointed in her. As the truck disappears into the night, she looks down into the little boy's eyes, who just smiles back at her. She then sighs and says, "Come on in, I think we may be able to help."

chapter seven

FIXED

By 10:05 pm two more families were there in need of help, the rumor of Rebecca's miracle was spreading. The second family to show up was a son with his 70yr old Alzheimer's suffering father and then a third family, a 32yr old recovering stroke victim being wheel chaired in by her father, Gary. Maggie's house was filling up, Jordan was tasked to make appetizers for the guest which he did without hesitation, and he wanted to test his appetizer cooking skills, anyway. Uncle Pete was back from dropping off Ed and watching Sports Center in the living room. Normally, that's what both Uncles would do when they came over, sit and argue over sports. Tonight, it was just Uncle Pete. Rebecca, Beverly, and Stella each were taking turns in the kitchen, explaining the phenomenon and making everyone feel at ease. Professor Lambkin was busy writing down everything that was occurring. He says to Maggie, "We are on the ground floor, of a historical event, that will change mankind forever. For posterity reasons alone, I need to write this all down." Maggie says, "Just make sure you get all the names right." Professor replies, "Oh I got them, especially yours Ms. Marshall." He winks at her as he says it. Maggie smiles and walks away shaking her butt...the Professor notices. "Oh, that reminds me I should text Dr. Rear, I'm sure she'd be interested in what's happening here." The professor says to himself as he takes his phone out of his pocket.

After his session with the Orb, the first family with the little boy with cancer is sent home. They are instructed not to wake the boy after he falls asleep and that he'd wake up when he was ready. No further instructions were given because no more was needed. The son with his elderly father also goes home. He was told the instructions and promises to carry his father to the bed without waking him, once they are home. The father and daughter decided to stay at the house since their drive was two hours away. With his daughter tucked away in the guest bed, Rebecca asks the father, "How did you know to come here, Gary?" Gary replies, "I'm always online looking for anything to help my Annie. I stumbled upon a miracle healing website and your picture was on it saying you were healed overnight from a birth deformity. There was an address, so I took a chance and brought my girl here in hopes of a miracle too.' As a tear rolled down his face, 'Annie's been through so much and she's so young, I just want my girl to have a chance at a normal, happy life. Thank you for taking us in and thank you for posting that on the internet." Gary hugs Rebecca, then goes and sits beside his daughter as Rebecca leaves the room, gently shutting the door behind her. In the kitchen Jordan is finishing washing dishes, he says, "I'm done for the night I'm going to my room to be a teenager." Maggie sitting at the table replies, "Son good job today, I'll take eggs benedict for breakfast." Jordan as he's walking out, looks at his mother and says, "Never made them before...challenge accepted. Gnite y'all." Everyone in the kitchen thanks and goodnights Jordan. Stella and Beverly decide to head home. Beverly says to Rebecca, "I'll be back here tomorrow, I have a feeling this is only the beginning and you're gonna need help." Rebecca nods. Beverly looks at Rebecca and says, "Thank you for being you." Rebecca smiles then Stella and Beverly leave. Uncle Pete takes the hint and also decides to head home, taking Professor Lambkin with him. The goodbye hug between Maggie and Professor Lambkin is a little longer than normal and there was a lot of hand rubbing. Rebecca and Uncle Pete shake their heads. Then Uncle Pete blurts out, "Okay awkward, time to go it's late and we have classes to teach tomorrow." The Professor looks at Maggie and eloquently says, "To experience the experience of this day, we look to the stars. But to feel the compassion of a loving home with a beautiful gracious host, I look to you. Thank you, Ms. Marshall and I bid you farewell, goodbye for now." Uncle Pete rolls his eyes and they both walk out of the house. Rebecca and Maggie look at each other and bust out laughing. Rebecca says, "Mamma, you got a man after you." Maggie replies, "Yea I know, one of many, it's a Marshall thing." She laughs. The women go into the kitchen and Rebecca says to her mom, "It's really bugging me, who put my picture up on the website, they put our address out there too. People are gonna start coming from all over now." Maggie replies, "Lemme tell you a little story. When I decided to become a nurse, it wasn't for fame or glory, it was to help those who need help. And in all my years, at different clinics and hospitals, I've witnessed one common thing. Illness will make a person desperate, make a sinner a saint, and a saint a sinner. People live on hope and people, no matter color or creed want to live." Maggie goes to the window and points to the barn and continues, "This thing that dropped from the sky and into our barn, is a way to give those living on hope... a life again. The Remaks didn't say it to me, but I felt it. They want to help us be better and help us become better. You are my daughter and if you tell me right now, you don't want any part of this, and we will stop right here, right now. Tell the Remaks to go find someone else and go about our lives like nothing happened." Maggie then holds both her daughters' hands and says lovingly, "Or, except you are special, and that's why they picked you. You have the power to help, the question now to you is, will you?" "Mom I'm only 18, I just graduated high school last week, I don't know if I'm ready to help, or save mankind. This just dropped in my lap... like now! Graduation presents are usually, a car or a trip to Hawaii. Not hey kid here's the power to save the world, hop to it." Rebecca says sarcastically. "Well it's your choice Becca, I'm here for you either way. Why don't you get some sleep and we'll talk some more about it tomorrow, I'll take the day off." Maggie says calmly. "Okay mom, I love you, thank you for being here for me." Rebecca says. Maggie replies, "For the rest of my life." Maggie kisses her daughter and shoo's her away saying, "Now go to bed I'll close up the house." Rebecca nods and smiles, then is just about to walk out when Jordan runs in screaming, "I suck playing with my eyes open, I'm getting my butt handed to me!" Rebecca says, "Well then play with your eyes closed." She shrugs her shoulders,

Jordan replies, "Now why didn't I think of that." Both kids leave the room as Maggie shakes her head.

That night Rebecca had her usual visit from the Remaks. She asked them what they wanted from her. They told her that her light was different, she was special unlike anyone on the planet, and she was a combination of everyone's light. And in that, she could connect with everyone, and if you can connect, you can understand each other. "And if you understand one another you can move towards a better future for your kind." They said "Just like by touching the Orb we now have a connection with you. You will have that, in time with everyone else." They also told her that healing her arm was not the only thing they did. They also made her stronger and smarter. "What was not good in you, is now better than it was before. What you could do before, you can do now better." In their words, "We fixed you."

Its 8:00 am on Monday, Rebecca's bedroom sits towards the front of the house. She slowly wakes up to the sounds of people chattering outside. Rebecca gets up and peers through her window curtains, she sees four cars parked along the road in front of her house. The occupants were all out of their vehicles chatting amongst themselves. She says to herself slightly overwhelmed, "Oh wow, more people to fix." She walks out of her room, down the hallway then left into the living room, then back towards the kitchen. When out of the corner of her eye, she sees her mom standing at the front door sipping on some coffee, looking at their future guest on the roadside. Maggie says, "They've been here since I woke up at seven. I think they are waiting for a sign that we're awake before they come knocking on the door... That's at least respectful of them. Did you think about what you wanted to do?" Rebecca replies, "Mom, the Remaks said they fixed me and made me stronger and better." Maggie turns around, looks at Rebecca and concerningly says, "Do you agree with them? Do you feel what they did to you, was a good thing? Do you regret it?" Rebecca looks down at the floor and says, "Maybe, I don't know." Just then there's a soft knock at the door, Maggie turns and opens the door, looks down, and sees the little boy from the night before with cancer. He stands looking at her with his big blue eyes and a smile from ear to ear, his brother and mother right behind him.

He proudly says, "My Name is Bobby Williams, I'm 10yrs old. The Remaks told me I was healed and I can feel it. I just wanted to come personally, to thank you and shake your hand." Maggie, taken back by his larger than life personality, puts her hand out and he shakes it with vigor. With his mom and brother looking on laughing with tears in their eyes, Bobby then looks at Rebecca and says, "You too." He walks up to Rebecca she puts her hand out, Bobby pauses then moves past her hand and gives her a big tight hug and whispers, "It's gone, I can feel it's all gone." Rebecca overwhelmed, looks at her mom and says, "I see what you're saying mom, It's not about me, It's about them." Bobby runs back to his family and his brother Quintin says, "We were on our way to the hospital to get him checked out when he insisted that we stop here first, so he could thank you. I also wanted to thank you, maybe I could one day take you out to lunch or something?" Quintin says looking at Rebecca. She smiles and is a little embarrassed being seen in her morning face. But she confidently replies to the handsome tall blonde young man, "Sure, I like lobster." He replies, "Me too." They smile and he and his mom thank Maggie for everything, then they leave. Maggie shuts the door Rebecca says, "Mom I can't do this without you." Maggie says, "I got you Becca." Rebecca takes a deep breath and says, "Okay let's fix some people." Maggie says, "Go wake up your brother then get yourself ready. I'll go tell our guest on the road, it'll be a little while longer." Rebecca goes to her room and gets her phone and texts, Hope and Beverly to come over soon as they can.

The kids shower and get ready for the day's company. But before that, Jordan prepares for his mother, Rebecca, and himself a spectacular eggs benedict breakfast. It's a hit and he pats himself on the back. Time is now about 8:40 am and Beverly drives up the driveway to the house. She picked up Hope and they walk into the house ready to work. Rebecca takes Hope to her room and asks her, "Did you post my picture and address on some website?" Hope replies surprised, "No! Why would I do that? Did someone do that?" Rebecca says, "yeah someone did and people showed up here last night because of it.' She looks out the window, 'I guess I wasn't prepared to have this out there so quickly." Hope says, "Becca, I'd never do that to you, without telling you. You know that?" Rebecca replies, "I know,

I'm sorry." Hope says, "Maybe someone from school or something. Either way, we are here to help you, whatever you need." Rebecca says, "Thanks." She smiles takes Hope's hand and walks out to the living room. Maggie and Beverly are waiting like soldiers ready for a command. Rebecca says, "Okay what's the game plan here?" Everyone looks ready to input their two cents, but Beverly is first out the gate. She says, "I'll escort people in, one family at a time. And explain to them what this is all about. If they have any questions, I can try and answer them, if not I'll send them to you." Rebecca says, "I like that." Hope says, "Okay, and when they get here, in the house, I'll ask them to donate whatever they can for your hospitality, as well as to help restore Flint. I'll need a big envelope for the money, and a pen and paper to write down their names." Rebecca says, "Good I like that too." Maggie says, "Becca, you and I should be the ones to take them to the barn." Rebecca replies, "Mom I agree. Okay great everyone has something." Jordan chimes in from the kitchen, "What about me?" As he walks through the kitchen door, "What do you want me to do?" Rebecca says, "Bake some cookies…a house always smells inviting with the aroma of cookies in the air." Jordan replies, "That too, I have never done before…challenge accepted." He smiles and winks at Hope then goes back into the kitchen. Rebecca says laughing, "I love my brother." Hope says smiling, "The boy has great taste." Rebecca says, "I love you all for doing this, let's go help some people." The four women huddle up and do a team chant, "Goooo Purple!!" They initially all go to the road and greet, the now six-car occupants waiting. The first family is escorted in, it's a 44yr old man with his mom and dad, and he's been blind from birth. After explaining everything and answering all the questions. They agree to go through with, "The Touch", as it would soon be called. The family leaves a generous donation of $500, Hope, Maggie, and Rebecca are beside themselves. Maggie and Rebecca happily take them through the kitchen and out the back door. While passing Jordan blurts out, "Hey Hey, you don't need to see to try these fresh out the oven cookies." Jordan extends a tray full of cookies to the passersby. They all take one on their way out, Jordan's ears are greeted with the sounds of delight. He replies, "That's right Chef Jordan in the house!" The day continues with families coming and leaving, well into the night.

Beverly within that time went to the store for the poster board. She made up signs and attached them to the roadside fence, to inform where to park and wait till working hours 9 am-10 pm. At 10:45 pm the gang is exhausted, they helped 24 families and currently, there were no cars waiting. The group gathered in the kitchen, Rebecca and Hope count the money donated, it come to a total of $8064. They all high-fived each other in celebration. Rebecca takes the money and pays $200 to everyone but herself and then donates $100 extra to her mom for food supplies. Rebecca says, "Right that leaves $7164 for Flint. Hope, tomorrow we need to find out who this money will be going to. And I'm afraid to say it, but we need help. Can you guys put the word out for volunteers, maybe?" Rebecca looks at their tired faces, "You did amazing today, thank you. If you don't want to show up tomorrow, I understand." Maggie says, "Becca I have to go to work tomorrow, I'm putting in my two weeks, because it seems, my daughter just put me out of a job.' She smiles, 'And into a better one." Rebecca smiles back she then says, "We need to make a website, hell our address is already out there, let's at least give them some correct information, right?" The gang agrees, Hope says, "So what should we call the website?" They all look at each other. Jordan says, "MarshallsHouse.com." They say, "Nah." Hope says "PurplePulse. com." Another, "Nah" echoes. Then Beverly says "Makers.com it's an anagram of the word Remaks." The group looks at each other and nods their heads, slow then faster and they clap to approval. Rebecca says, "I love it, okay I'll work on that before bed. So, what time you wanna meet here tomorrow, 9 am?" Hope and Beverly agree, Rebecca hugs them and then they leave. Jordan retires to his room and Rebecca looks at her mom and says, "We did good today, right?" Maggie replies, "Baby, Becca we did better than good, tomorrow a blind man will see, a child will walk, a deaf woman will hear for the first time in her life. So many beautiful changes will happen, to all, not just the ones that touched the Orb. But also, to the people that cared for them and brought them here to see you. You handled yourself so well, you are a natural caregiver." She hugs her daughter, "I won't see you in the morning when you wake up, but I'll try and come home soon as I can to help." Rebecca says, "Thanks, mom. I'm tired I think I'll work on the website tomorrow." "Okay baby."

Maggie says. Rebecca goes to her room and fully clothed crawls into bed and falls asleep. That night the Remaks flooded her dreams with memories of their planet and its beauty. From Panda Elephants to giant butterflies big as eagles with multiple colors. There were mini giraffes with zebra stripes and unicorns that were pink running in blue grass fields. Swimming in the oceans, there are enormous whales and dolphins gliding through the current. This is all peaceful and pleasant, Rebecca has a smile on her face as she sleeps.

chapter eight

FLINT

Rebecca's alarm goes off at 8:00 am and again she can hear the chattering of people. She looks through the window and sees her mom standing out of her car, yelling at TV crews. There are news vans all up and down the road. Rebecca calls her mom on her cell phone. Maggie answers, "Hi baby, you okay?" "Yes, I'm fine, what are you doing, I see you yelling at people?" Rebecca replies. "No, I'm yelling at these damn news people harassing people that are here asking for help. I told them to stay off my damn property and that we'll give them a press briefing later when I get home. So, don't you entertain anyone from the media till I get home, okay.' sternly she reiterates, 'You hear me?" "Okay, mom." Rebecca replies. "Alright I love you, be home soon," Maggie says as she hangs up gets in her car and speeds off to work. Rebecca walks down the hall and bangs on Jordan's door, "Wake up chef!" she says. She goes in the bathroom to pee and as she is doing so, she's group texting Hope and Beverly about the madhouse that awaits them. Beverly texts back that her mom is coming to help and Hope says she has someone also.

The women show up at 8:46 am, Hope exits the car as soon as it stops and runs to Rebecca who has opened the front door for them. Hope screams, "Oh My God!! The cars go for like a mile long, and there are news people everywhere, turn on the TV." All the girls enter the house and close the front door. They turn on the TV and see, on every local news channel, there's a reporter, reporting a story about, "Purple Alien Invasion". Jordan says, "Yo, I'm gonna be famous." "Whoa, slow it down there speed racer." Rebecca retorts. "This ain't no reality TV show." Just then, a car comes driving up the driveway, parks in front of the house, and two boys get out. Rebecca says, "Who the hell is this?" Hope says, "It's some extra help." Rebecca gives a snide look to Hope and Hope smiles. Hope opens the door and its Quintin and his friend Damon the quarterback from their high school team. Quintin says, "Hi, Hope said you guys needed some help, so I jumped at the chance, and I brought a friend, this is Damon, where do you want us." Damon greets everyone, he's a good looking, tall well-built kid with long dreads. He says to Rebecca, "Yea, hey I can get more help if you want, you just say the word and I can have twenty guys down here, pronto." Beverly nudges Rebecca and whispers, "Say the word." Rebecca whispers out of the corner of her mouth, "Keep it in your pants, Anderson." She then looks over to Damon and says, "Are you serious? Do it, we are gonna need all the help we can get today. Has everyone eaten yet?" The group gives mixed answers. Rebecca says, "Okay let's do this then, Jordan go make some finger foods, and when they're ready let us know. Beverly and Damon you guys are on point, you escort the families in, and at the same time, you'll be out there to see when Damon's boys show up. Hope will be here in the living room doing donations, Stella do you want to help out my brother or me in the barn?" Stella replies, "I'll help Jordan, I got some recipes to show him." Rebecca says, "Okay great, well I guess, Quintin you're with me in the barn." Rebecca blushes and says quickly, "I mean you're helping me in the barn." The gang chuckles and Quintin says, "I'll go in the barn anytime, with you." He smiles at her and Rebecca laughs and says, "Oh, and everybody, don't say anything to the news reporters, we'll handle them later. Well like Tommy said, let's do it, its go time!" They do a team hand cheer again and break to their respective places. Beverly and Damon are walking out to the road and Beverly says to Damon, "You know, I saw your last game, you caught your own pass that bounced off the linemen and ran it in for a touchdown...pretty cool." Damon replies, "Yea would have been nice if we won that game though." Beverly says, "Yea I bet, don't fret, let's see how you make it through today, you do that, and you're a winner in my book." She smiles and looks at him. He looks at her and takes out his phone and takes a pic of the line of cars and says, "This is for real huh?" Beverly says, "Well they ain't all out here waiting for toilet paper. You call your boys, I'll handle this first family, and don't talk to the press." She says as they approach the first car in line.

In about an hour, fourteen of Damon's teammates come to help. Beverly so happens, found out she is really good at organizing and delegating people. First off, she puts two, two-man teams on each end of the property by the road, so no one would sneak onto the property. The land was flat and open, so it was easy to see if someone was trying to get to the barn. She then went through five cars at a time, deciding who was a priority, then sticking one of the guys with them, to escort them in, when it was their turn. The others would rotate with the five, so no one was being overworked with breaks in-between. Beverly was telling the families only enough to put them at ease and make them feel, that they didn't waste their time coming. She explained that all their important questions would be answered inside. She kept Damon at her side, so he could learn the ropes, he was cool, she'd never hung out with a jock before. It wasn't as bad, as she thought it would be, in other words, she liked Damon's style.

Inside, Hope was doing her part collecting donations, she was particularly happy because she loved the city where she grew up , and with all the money they were taking in, just meant they'd be one step closer to restoring it. Jordan and Stella were having a blast cooking together. Stella was once a short-order cook, and she was showing Jordan some shortcuts to preparing and serving. Rebecca and Quintin were being as understanding and compassionate to each case as possible. Every encounter is bittersweet and the Touchers, the name Rebecca called them now, are quickly put at ease after they hear Rebecca's story and Quintin's brother's story... Jordan and Stella's cookies also help.

Around noon Maggie came home, she brought two of her patients with her. One with AIDS and the other with Parkinson's disease. She walks in the house with her two guests and puts them both in one of the guest rooms. Hope's hosting the next Toucher and her husband in the living room as Rebecca and Quintin enter the backdoor after finishing up with the last Toucher. Maggie waves her daughter over and says, "I wrote up what you should say to the news later. When your grandmother and grandfather were killed, the news came by and they reported a story, totally different from what happened. I don't want that happening to you." Rebecca says, "When do you want me to do this?" Maggie replies, "Now if you want, I took off the rest of the day. I brought home two of my patients. They have no one and need help." She's abruptly interrupted by Beverly bursting in the door screaming "The Mayor's here!" Everyone's face goes blank and Maggie says, "Becca, you're on…" Rebecca says, "Holy shit, okay mom you take over for me please, Beverly bring the Mayor here to the living room, but no reporters." She looks around the living room franticly. "Okay, we'll put him on the couch. Hope… sister it's your time to shine, pitch to him how we make this work for Flint. I'll handle the rest.' She pauses and says shaking her head, 'I sure hope he's not a weasel politician."

Beverly enters the house with Mayor McBride and his female assistant. The mayor is a stocky grey-haired man, six feet tall in an imported Italian suit. With a big mayoral grin, he says, "Good afternoon everyone, I am Marty McBride, and this is my assistant Karen, pardon us interrupting your day. I heard of a miraculous thing happening here and I decided to come have a look. Who is Rebecca?" Rebecca raises her hand and says, "I am Mr. Mayor." She walks up to him shakes his hand and directs him to the couch and says, "Would you like a seat?" He and his assistant sit, and she introduces her mom, brother, Stella, Quintin, and lastly Hope. Hope sticks her hand out for a handshake and says, "It's a pleasure to meet you sir," He shakes her hand firmly and says, "So you have a healing alien Orb in the barn I heard? Is that true?" Hope says, "Yes sir we do and with your help, we'd like to use it to help the people of Flint and anyone else with it." He says, "Absolutely I'm all for helping the community. Can I see it?" Rebecca says, "Sure, but first I have some things to explain to you before that happens. Let's just call it, your orientation briefing.' Rebecca turns to direct attention to the awaiting couple, 'This lovely person is next, with their permission, and you'll be able to witness in full effect." Rebecca smiles at the waiting couple, and says, "Hi I'm Rebecca Marshall, thank you for coming. How may we help you?"

The woman explains she is suffering from breast cancer. Rebecca calmly says, "I think you came to the right place. Did you already speak to Hope?" The husband and woman nod yes. Rebecca then says, "Okay thank you for your donation. I'm going to tell the story to you now, do you mind if the mayor listens in?" The couple shake their heads and the woman says, "No I don't mind." Rebecca says, "Alrighty then, let's get started." The mayor listens as she tells the story. He seems interested as much as any self-interested politician would be. After she completes her story, she answers the usual questions. Will it hurt? Was she scared? How does she feel? And so on. Finally, it's the moment of truth, Rebecca asks the woman if she's still willing to go through with it. The woman says, "What do I have to lose, the doctors only gave me six months." Rebecca gives her a look of comfort, and says, "Tomorrow you won't even know how to spell the word cancer." Rebecca smiles holds out her hand for the woman and says, "What's, your name?" The woman says, "My name is Wendy." Rebecca says, "Pleased to meet you Wendy." She then walks her out of the backdoor. The husband, mayor, assistant, Maggie, Quintin, and even Hope follows to the barn. You can hear cameras snapping pics, and reporters yelling questions from the roadside. The group enters the barn through the side door, as to not let the lookie-loos see from the road. The grass has now pretty much covered the whole floor of the barn. The mayor's assistant starts recording it all on her phone. Maggie says laughing, "Becca I guess you need to take Caroline for a ride in here." Rebecca says, "I know right." The group circles the Orb, the mayor, and the first-time onlookers are all mesmerized by the pulsing purple light. Rebecca softly says, "Wendy, are you ready?" Wendy looks at her husband and grabs his hand. She gazes over everyone, and sees them all smiling back at her, especially Maggie, who is shaking her head and giving Wendy the double thumbs-up, as she whispers, "It's amazing!" As usual, after touching the Orb Wendy falls back, they pick her up, Rebecca has Quintin and Maggie walk the couple out. Rebecca says to the mayor, "That's it, tomorrow Wendy will wake up cancer-free. We can heal every one of everything, forever. What we need from you, since you're here, is help." She looks at Hope and gestures for her to go. Hope looks at the mayor and plays to his ego. She says, "How bad do you want to be re-elected?" He says, "I'm listening." Hope continues, "We need Port-a-Potty's, Food trucks and 24hr security, maybe even a shuttle service, from hotels to us and back. Oh, and tax-exempt status. In return, we are willing to give a large portion of the money donated, to help rebuild Flint. But it must only be used, to rebuild and help the people of Flint. This, I'm sure would ensure your re-election and allow us to keep doing what we are doing.' Hope with a softer innocent tone, 'Mr. Mayor, with the money we generate here, we can save Flint and make it better than it ever was before." The mayor takes a moment, rubs his chin, and replies, "Well I can help out with some of that of course, but I will have to coordinate with the governor, this is a little above my paygrade. I do see the potential of this... it is worldwide." He looks down at the ground and to his assistant then to Rebecca and says, "So you're telling me, there are no side effects to this at all?" Rebecca says, "None I've found, my mind hasn't been taken over, there's no alien being controlling me, telling me to kill all the humans...yet." She laughs. The mayor hesitantly laughs too and says, "Can I touch it?" His assistant instantly grabs his arm pulling him back. The mayor looks at Karen and says, "Its ok." Rebecca says, "I did and I'm better for it." The mayor stoops down and then everyone hears a man with a bullhorn broadcast, "Stay away from this place, it is a place of divine evil! Extraterrestrial magic that does not belong here on our planet. Do not touch it, for if you do, you become, something else. Not one of god's children, not one of your ancestors like Adam or Eve, not even the same person you were at birth, but something else. A child of the purple light, a child of the purple devil." They all go and slide open the main barn door to see who the menacing voice is, Hope in shock says, "Oh my god that's your..." Rebecca says, "Uncle Ed." Uncle Ed has parked his car on the property just on the inside of the driveway entrance and is standing on his roof with a bullhorn in one hand and the bible in the other, voicing his displeasure with what was going on. He then turns and sees the group in the barn and calls out the mayor. "Ah... Mr. Mayor, Mr. Marty McBride, I'm not surprised to see you here, where I would be surprised to see you are in church. But I know you're too busy on Sundays running around with all those women, while your pregnant wife is left alone at home. And we know about your deal—makings with the corporate lobbyist, to sell out the people of our community. I see you Mr. Mayor." The mayor gets nervous and grabs his assistant and they scurry back to the house. Rebecca and Hope start walking towards Uncle Ed. As they pass the front of the house Maggie exits the front door, slamming the screen door behind her. She is walking briskly towards Ed. Ed keeps voicing his godly opinion unto the roadside dwellers. As Rebecca is walking up, she looks at Beverly like, "Why didn't you stop him?" She looks back at her like, "He's your uncle, duh." Maggie slams her hand on the hood of the car and yells at him, "Get your ass down here, cause you don't want me to come up there." Ed gets off the roof then onto the hood of his car and sits there. He pans his arms left to right and yells so all can hear, "I am saving these people from what they don't know. I couldn't save my own family, but I can try and save these fine people. I was the last to find out about this cause you knew I would oppose." Maggie says, "No, it wasn't even a thought of mine. I touched it and it healed me. My daughter and son touched it and it healed them that is what I was thinking about. How is what we are doing, different than what you do every day? You know what the real difference is… what we are doing works, and you're mad about that? You're mad that my son can see, my daughter has use of her arm. You'd rather them be cripple and blind. Is that it? Ed, you wanna do this shit, okay fine mom and dad would be proud. Go ahead preach, and guilt everyone who needs help away from here." Maggie then looks at the crowd and yells out, "I won't stop you, but for all you people that do stay, you are welcome to come in for help." She looks at the large mass of people that have formed on the roadside, there are at least 200. Their phones have recorded it all, and the media was live, broadcasting it worldwide. Maggie looks at Beverly and says, "You keep bringing in whoever wants to, you hear?" Beverly nods. Maggie turns around and starts walking briskly back to the house. Hope and Rebecca turn and do the same. Hope says to Rebecca, "Well I guess you won't have to give that press briefing now." Rebecca says, "Good, cause I don't know how you top that?" As the girls are walking back to the house, they see the mayor's car with him in it, quickly passing them by in the opposite direction. He doesn't look or wave, and Uncle Ed gives him another verbal beat down with the bullhorn as he leaves.

The girls get back to the house and see Maggie is still mad. She's in the kitchen drinking a glass of wine. Maggie rarely drinks, so for her to do so meant things were not right. Maggie shoots the glass of wine down in one gulp and with restraint calmly says, "Guys let's get back to work. We have two people in the guest room the need our help. Quintin, Rebecca let's go." Maggie flips a switch and acts like nothing's wrong, Rebecca knows better, she knows her mom will confront Ed again in private, and to stay out of it. She helps her mom with her two patients out to the barn, it takes a little coaxing because of the recent commotion, but they get there. When they return, they put Maggie's patients in the guest room to sleep it off. Rebecca, Maggie and Quintin walk into the living room for the next Toucher, when Beverly burst in the front door again. Rebecca says, "The mayor's back?" Beverly says breathing heavily, "No worse! The government!" Rebecca says, "Oh shit! Hope take the money to my mom's room. Somebody, record this." Jordan and Quintin take out their phones and start recording. Hope hurries the envelope into the room. Just then, four men in black suits walk up onto the porch and knock on the door trim. One peeks his head in the already open door and says in a very monotone way, "Good day, I'm Mr. Jenkins with the Federal Bureau of Investigations. May we come in?" Maggie says, "Be my guest. How are you today, how may we help you sirs?" Jenkins says, "Oh I think you know why we are here." He then introduces the other three gentlemen "This is Mr. Smith, Mr. Stewart, and Mr. Rogers all with the bureau as well." They all look like bad rip-offs of Agent Smith from the movie The Matrix to Rebecca, and she giggles. Agent Jenkins dismissively looks at her briefly and continues addressing Maggie. "A little birdie told us, that there's some sort of meteorite in your barn that has the ability to heal people... Is that so?" Maggie contemptuously says, "What if it does?" Jenkins looks at his men, then back at Maggie and dickishly says, "Well ma'am, you could be messing with something more dangerous than you know. And, we've even heard, you've had physical contact with this meteorite. That may not have been a smart move on your part." Quintin and Jordan are slowly positioning on each side of the living room video recording the conversation. Jenkins looks at the young men raises his hand and says, "You don't need to record us, son, we're not here to cause any trouble." Rebecca says suspiciously, "I don't believe you." Jenkins says, "And who are you?" Rebecca confidently says, "I'm Rebecca." Jenkins replies, "Oh, you're the one?" She replies, "Yes, I'm the one." Jenkins makes his way through the living room to Rebecca and puts his hand out to shake hers. She returns the gesture, with a firmer squeeze than he was expecting. Jenkins quirky smiles as he takes his hand back and shakes it off. He says, "You've got a firm grip there. I've heard some stories about you, your arm looks completely normal." Rebecca says, "I know like brand new, huh?" As Rebecca shows off her arm and says, "See nothing dangerous here. Just a fully functioning arm." Jenkins asks, "So this healed right after you touched it?" Rebecca unsmilingly replies, "Yes. Do you gentlemen want to get out of my house?" She bites her lip then repeats, "Would you gentlemen like to get out and go see it, I mean, that is why you're here, right?" Jenkins nods and says, "Yes, we would." Rebecca leads the men through the kitchen, even offering some cookies to which none of them partakes. Quintin and Jordan follow recording every moment as everyone follows. They get to the barn overlooking the Orb, but it's not pulsing, it's just glowing. Everyone that knows, see this but don't say anything, instead, they are just looking at Rebecca for an explanation. She sees them, and reacts with a slight shrug of her shoulders while making a face, then looks at Jenkins and says, "Well here it is. We done? I got people to help?" Jenkins says, "Yea about that. That stops now!" Maggie instantly says, "Okay enough of this bullshit. You gotta go, I don't care what agency you work for, you ain't gonna come on my property and tell me what the hell to do!" Jenkins says, "Ma'am please don't make this difficult, this is for your safety as well as the nation." One of the men, Mr. Smith moves towards to grab Beverly and she pushes him with such force that he goes flying back out of the barn. Jenkins says, "What the fuck was that! You just assaulted a federal officer!" Beverly says calmly, "No sir he intruded on my space and I rejected his advances... he's not my type." She glares. Rebecca says, "Sir go..." Jenkins and his men back out, picking up their fallen agent along the way. Jenkins says, "We will not be so nice next time you see us, and you will see us... soon." Rebecca says, "I'm your Huckleberry... And Mr. Jenkins I suggest next time you come back, do something good. Bring someone who is sick and in need of help. Do not come to try to take the Orb, or harm any of us. You will fail." Jenkins stares into Rebecca's eyes and sees she is not joking. The men get in their black suburban and speed off the property. Maggie takes out her phone and dials. Rebecca asks, "Who you calling?" Maggie says, "Pete." Pete answers, "Hello." Maggie starts talking as the group is making their way back to the house. Maggie says with urgency, "Pete, I need you to go now to the governor's house in Lansing and do whatever you have to do to get him to my house now, it's an emergency. I'm not asking I'm telling you. Love you, bye." Maggie hangs up and says, "We need some political clout, why not go straight to the top." Rebecca then says, "Good mom, I hope he comes through for us. Meantime, we must get as many people cured, and on our side, before Mr. Jenkins ever gets back. I'm pulling an all-nighter, you all don't have to stay, but if you do, I thank you in advance." She does a Namaste thank you gesture, then turns around and heads to the roadside waiting room. Beverly, Quintin, Stella, and Maggie all follow her, Hope and Quintin go to the house.

The night drags on, at around 11:50 pm, they have helped about thirty people. The gangs are all tired and living on caffeine. The only ones left helping at this time, are Hope, Beverly, Stella, Maggie, and Quintin. There are, however, two additional volunteers, the two patients that Maggie brought home, their names are John and Penny. After sleeping most of the day, when they woke, the usual happened. Just like the rest of the new Touchers, they had an overwhelming zest for life. Therefore, they offered to help. Felt it was their duty, in a manner of paying it forward so to speak. Rebecca directs the new blood to the roadside, to aid in escorting. Their enthusiasm of just being healed, helped reassure new visitors. The football players had all left, but most said they'd be back tomorrow, and some with people they knew needed help. Hope was manning the money the whole day. Between break periods of new Touchers, she jotted down notes and came up with a F.A.Q. for the people visiting, so they could get familiar with everything and save time. She kept hearing a lot of the same questions over and over, and to her, this made sense to do. She printed up like fifty copies and gave them to John and Penny, to pass out to each awaiting car. Hope told Rebecca about what she did, she agreed with the idea and gave her, her laptop to create a webpage and add it in. Rebecca then hugs her tight, and said "I love you, you're my best friend, and I can't imagine doing this with anyone else but you, thanks sis." Hope lovingly replies, "Me too sis… You better soak up all of this ginger you can, because next semester I'm college-bound." Rebecca says, "Get that degree girl, with your ambition you'll be governor one day." Hope says, "Screw that…I'll be President!" Rebecca replies, "You right!" they both laugh.

Maggie was just getting out of the bathroom and heading to get another cup of coffee when her phone rang. It's an unfamiliar number, so she lets it go to voicemail. Then it rings again, she answers it, it's Professor Lambkin, he says, "Hello Maggie, sorry to call you so late, I hope you don't mind, but I got your number from your brother. I want to tell you something that I think you'll want to know. Who's all there?" Maggie confused says, "Well pretty much everyone you met at the house the other day." The professor exclaims, "Perfect! Well get everyone together and put me on speakerphone." Maggie rounds the group up, they huddle around the phone in the living room. Maggie says, "Alright professor, the gang's all here, and you're on speaker. What do you have to tell us?" The professor says, "First off, hello all. I am so excited to tell you about something that we recently discovered. I met with my colleague Dr. Rear, who is one of the top minds in the field of Genetics and Hematology. I told her what happened to me and she insisted on taking a blood sample. Are you guys curious as to what the results are so far?" There are multiple "Yeses and acknowledgeable grunts" that reply. The professor says, "Dr. Rear has run twenty-two individual tests currently, and she found that my blood cells are immune to every disease she's introduced. From cancer to the common cold. What do you guys think about that?" Rebecca says, "Really?" The professor says, "Really, and I'm not done. Here's the kicker, my cells are deteriorating at half the rate. That means, I'm aging at half my normal. It's the fountain of youth people." He yells out "Eureka!" In the house, there's a peaceful quiet that rests for a brief moment, followed by a roar of cheers and exuberance. Hope and Quintin are the only ones that have not touched the Orb, but in spirit, they commemorate along with everyone else. Quintin says to Hope, "Maybe we should jump on this bandwagon too?" Hope says, "You go ahead, I'm not quite ready yet… But it does look fun." Quintin goes over to Rebecca holds her hands and starts dancing about with her. Hope watches on smiling, but inside, she feels jealousy, not towards Rebecca, but towards Quintin. Maggie stops the celebration and tells the professor thank you for letting us know. The professor says, "My pleasure, it would be a greater pleasure for me to take you to dinner, next time I'm down there." Everyone hears that and goes quiet, Maggie pleasantly responds, "I'd like that Professor…The next time you're here then, it's a date." The professor replies, "I'll be there tomorrow night." Laughter fills the house, and Maggie replies, "I'll see you then tomorrow professor. Goodnight." The professor says, "Goodnight Ms. Marshall." After a couple of minutes of teasing, Maggie settles all the mockery and gets everyone back to the job at hand. On the porch, the next person in need has been waiting, it's a little boy with a disfigured arm like Rebecca had. Rebecca stoops down to his eye level and says "Hi, my name is Rebecca. What's yours?" The little boy shyly says, "I'm Charlie." As he squeezes his teddy bear into his chest. Rebecca says, "What a cute bear, what's his name?" Charlie says, "His name is Butter." Rebecca giggles, "Hi Butter, Charlie did you know my arm was just like yours?" Charlie replies "Really?" Rebecca says, "Yep, sure was. But then I touched the purple light and the next day it was all better." Charlie sadly says, "I want to be all better, other kids make fun of me." Rebecca looks at Charlie's parents standing behind him, then back at Charlie and says, "Don't ever let those mean kids get you down. Charlie, you are amazing and you're going to do astonishing things in your life. Don't ever let mean people, mean anything to you. Okay?" Charlie nods his head. Rebecca takes his good arm and leads him to the kitchen and says, "Want a cookie?" Charlie nods again Rebecca smiles and says, "Okay, how about we all walk out to the barn." Charlie says, "Okay, can Butter have a cookie too?" "Sure," Rebecca replies. His parents smile and roll their eyes when Rebecca looks at them.

As they enter the barn, the Orb is pulsing bright, the barn strobes like a nightclub again. The freshly grown grass has invited in a bunch of fireflies, which are blinking and fluttering around. It looks like a little Garden of Eden. Charlie sees all of this and Rebecca says, "This was all done for you, the Orb isn't usually this bright, you must be really special Charlie.' Charlie smiles. 'Okay, are you ready?" Charlie looking a little scared nods. Rebecca softly says, "Alright, when you touch it you're gonna feel an amazing feeling throughout your body, but its okay, that's part of it. Then you can go home. Okay, Charlie?" Charlie hesitantly says, "Okay." His parents help him touch the Orb and catch him when falls back. Charlie is giggling, frighteningly. Rebecca talks to the parents and informs them what to do, and what's going to happen next, as they walk out of the barn. At the end, she asks for a donation in which they give $1500. She thanks them and goes back to the house for the next Toucher. She keeps going like this, till there are no more cars waiting. It's 4:15 am on Wednesday. She locks up the barn and heads in, everyone else except for Hope and Beverly were gone, or sleeping. Beverly wave's goodnight and goes to sleep in one of the guest rooms, Hope assumes her spot next to Rebecca in her bed. The girls mumble goodnight to each other, and as soon as they hit the bed they were out.

In Rebecca's dream that night, the Remaks visit their chosen one, and though her body is exhausted, her mind is very alert. They come to her as she is sitting on a hilltop cliff, overlooking the yellow oceans of Res. The white sun is setting on the horizon, as the shimmer of gold speckles, cascade throughout the vast ocean against an emerald green sky backdrop. The Remaks unison voice asks, "How are you, Rebecca?" She asks, "Why did the Orb pulse brighter with the little boy?" They respond, "The Orb reacts to how you are feeling. You wanted the boy to feel at ease, and the Orb responded. Whenever the Orb is close, it will always be an extension of you. Just like when you felt threatened by Jenkins, it was channeling your feelings. If you had reacted, it would have as well." She takes a deep breath and says, "I'm in over my head, aren't I?" They reply, "No from our standpoint, you are "holding your own" as your people would say." She replies, "So at what time were you going to tell me, that we are immortal after we touch the Orb." The Remaks say, "We wanted your life expectancy to be a surprise and no, you are not immortal. You will still die, and you can still be killed, you just have a more prolonged life than before. If you get cut or shot, you will bleed, though you will heal extremely fast, if you are saved. But no earthly disease will ever cause you harm." Rebecca says, "That's good to know. So, are there any other hidden gems you didn't tell me? Why did you say earthly disease?"

The Remaks change the surroundings to a black void. The Remak being appears in front of Rebecca and says, "You are our chosen one. In order to fix you, we had to give us to you, in this light form we are not affected by your earthly sicknesses so, therefore, neither are you now." Rebecca takes a moment and suspiciously replies, "Somethings not right. You're not in the Orb anymore are you?" The Remaks reply, "No, we are not, we are in you." She pauses, then amazed says, "So, you are healing these people through me...through the Orb?" The unison voice says, "Yes." Rebecca irritated says, "You are using me, aren't you? You say you're here to help us, but really, we are helping you, survive. You lack the will to defend and protect yourselves, so you come up with a brilliant idea to attach yourself to us. Hey, why not, we look like an inferior species, let's take over the humans. Am I right? Leach off our existence for your own. Tell me the truth, are you going to take over our bodies?" The voices say, "We are sorry if you feel we deceived you. You were our best opportunity, amongst thousands of lifeforms to continue surviving. And no, we will not take over your bodies, but instead fuse with it, a sort of hybrid." Rebecca interrupts, "Wait!! So does that mean our babies will not look like us?!!" The Remaks reply, "In time, gradually yes, our physical form will evolve into a mix, between both our species." Rebecca angrily shouts, "Why didn't you tell me this from the beginning?!! My Uncle Ed was right then. Oh my god, what have I done... What have I done?" Sobbing she says, "I convinced all these people to do this. I'm so stupid, I should have known better. What did I do?" The Remaks try and ease her disappointment by saying, "Rebecca, if you so ask we will leave your planet. We will also remove our subconscious from the people affected. We are not here to invade just to save what's left of our species. We believe our bonding will be beneficial to us both. There's so much we can teach each other. We feel honored to be a part of you. The people you have touched are forever changed, for the better. They then put up multiple screens, of all the people she's helped. Bobby's with his family playing and happy, she sees the old man with Alzheimer's, cured reliving past memories, the woman with the stroke was now walking and talking enjoying her life. She sees the inner lives of everyone she's helped so far, happy, and their loved ones enjoying them. The being says, "Rebecca, this is what you've done." The Remaks slowly disappear, and everything goes black as they leave Rebecca, to rest on her own.

chapter nine

GREEN FLASH

Beverly wakes up before everyone else and goes into the kitchen, for some water. She sees two men lurking around the barn, trying to get inside. She calmly goes outside, and makes her way to the barn, picking up the aluminum bat along the way. The intruders are so concentrated, on getting a glimpse of what's inside the barn, they don't notice her walking up. Beverly stands ten feet behind them and sternly says, "Did you gentlemen not see the sign I put out by the road? Trespassers and solicitors will be dealt with, swiftly." The two men turn around, they have cameras hanging off their necks. One man rudely says, "Do you live here?" Beverly gives a testy reply, "Yes I do, now get off this property ASAP." He replies snarky as he walks up to her "And if we don't, you'll hit me with that bat and I'll sue you." Beverly says, "Um, the bats not for me, it's for you." She throws the bat to him and he catches it. Eyes raised she says, "Oh, you want to hit me with a bat huh?" Beverly lunges towards the man, he drops the bat and screams, and she grabs him by his shirt collar and flings him behind her towards the road. The second man puts his hands up and says, "I'm going, don't touch me, I'm going." Both run off the property, and the media sitting roadside get it all on all tape. Beverly nonchalantly waves at the news crews as she walks back to the house. When Beverly walks into the kitchen, Maggie is there to greet her, she asks, "What was that all about?" Beverly smiles and says, "It's cool, just some adorning fans that wanted my attention, you know, just giving the fans what they ask for." Maggie says, "You see the four cop cars out there today?" Beverly says, "Yea, don't worry I have a way with the law, I'll talk to them about our situation in a bit. Maggie says, "Alright then, you, my head girl is in charge!" Beverly says, "You Right!"

Rebecca's alarm goes off at 8 am, she's very slow to get up. Faced with her new knowledge, she's not as enthused to carry on with this plight as before. She lays there staring at the ceiling fan, spinning round and round, it's almost hypnotic. She wishes none of this had ever happened to her. She finally gets up out of bed and sees Hope was already up and gone. She walks into the kitchen and sees her mom dressed for work, and Jordan washing the dishes from the breakfast he made. John and Penny are eating at the table, along with Beverly and Hope. Maggie says, "Good morning super trooper, how'd you sleep?" Rebecca slumps down at the table, starts crying, and says, "I think I messed up mom, the Remaks didn't tell us the whole truth. They don't just heal us... If we touch the Orb, they become part of us, like physically too... Like forever. And worse, it's not them, it's me. I control the Orb, I've been controlling it this whole time. I'm the one that heals everyone. I'm the one that infects people with the Remaks. I never realized the consequences of touching it. I just thought we were all just gonna be healed. I feel so gullible... so stupid. Mom, Uncle Ed was right we are no longer completely human anymore." Maggie sighs and says, "Becca don't beat yourself up for following your heart baby. We all touched it for our own reasons, your brother can see now because that, he doesn't regret it. We were all naïve to think this gift, was without a price. I had a feeling they had an ulterior reason for bestowing this upon us, from their story. Whether it be prolonging their survival or ours. But, after seeing what they did for my kids, I think it's worth it. The question for the rest of the world now will be, is it worth it for them. I think it is. I haven't had contact with the Remaks, since that first night, they chose you to keep a connection with, for a reason. They believe in you, I believe in you...we believe in you." The whole gang huddles around Rebecca and gives her a massive hug. Rebecca wipes away her tears and says, "Thanks so much for your support guys. Hey, mother always knows best, Right?" Maggie nods and winks at her daughter. Beverly says, "You gave me purpose and you gave my mother a second chance. From my heart, I am your ride or die…" Hope goes to say something too when there's a knock on the front door. Maggie opens the door, its Damon and the football team, at least twenty guys this time. Damon says to Beverly, "Am I the winner in your book yet?" Beverly says, "Kinda, you think you can run the road show today?" Damon says, "No sweat." She smiles. Rebecca calls to everyone from the kitchen "Listen, everybody thanks for coming, but before we start today I need to address everyone, I mean like a press briefing, so I'm gonna take a shower, and then I'll be out. You guys just hang out till then." Maggie says, "Becca I gotta go to work and drop off John and Penny, but I'll be back soon as I can, okay, love you." Rebecca smiles a sad smile at her mom and goes in the bathroom. As Maggie is walking out she says, "Oh, and you guys give my son a break today, when you're hungry lemme know and I'll have pizzas delivered." Jordan says, "Wooohooo, free day, hey Hope want some company today." Hope chuckles and says, "Sure, you can help me design the website." Hope looks at Beverly and says, "You wanna go out there and let the press know she's ready to talk to them… without the bat this time." Hope and Beverly laugh. Beverly throws her hands up says, "Hey, I was just trying to make it an even fight… for them." Damon asks Beverly, "What's up with the bat?" Beverly whispers to his ear, "I'll tell you about it later." She then starts walking out of the house and yells, "Hey everybody, follow me to the front yard. Damon's gonna tell you what to do, and I gotta go get the media ready."

A half hour later, Rebecca walks out of her room, trying to make the best impression she can. She is wearing a long summer dress, it has yellow flowers with little red lady bugs on it. Maggie bought it for her 17th birthday. They searched five stores downtown, for the right dress to celebrate her special day. Hope says, "Aw, I was hoping you'd choose that one, you wear it so well. Rebecca says, "Thank you, because you know I'd rather be in shorts and a t-shirt, this itches. Alright, let's do this." The front screen door creaks as they open it. They walk out onto the porch and all eyes are on Rebecca. Hope sensing Rebecca's nervousness says, "Hold my hand I'll walk with you." It's about 150ft to the road, they can see Beverly waiting for them at the driveway entrance. She's made a makeshift podium out of 3 milk crates, wrapping paper, and duct tape. Quintin is there also, along with the whole football team. Rebecca takes center stage, there are twenty microphones and voice recorders from the media laying on the top crate. With her support group standing behind her, she nervously says, "Hello everyone, good morning. My name is Rebecca Marshall, I am here to tell you, about the events, which have happened these last few days. I know you must have a lot of questions, and I'll try and answer them. But please wait till I'm through.' Rebecca looks behind her again, to see the faces of encouragement. She takes a deep breath and says, 'A few nights ago, early Sunday morning, I was getting a drink of water in my kitchen, and I heard a boom, then saw something crash into our barn. I went to see what it was, and it turned out to be some kind of purple pulsing object. It was embedded in the ground in the barn. I didn't know what it was, or where it came from, at the time. I touched it, I don't know why, but I did. Many of you don't know me, I was born with my left arm disfigured. It remained that way all my life... All my life, until I touched that purple Orb. I fell asleep shortly after touching it, I had a dream that night, and in the dream, I met the beings in the Orb, they call themselves, Remaks. They told me about themselves, and that they were here to help us, and I believed them. You see, all my life, wherever I went, I was talked about and pointed at. I tried to not let it bother me, making the best of my circumstance, but really, I've never felt, normal. And it hurt. All I ever wished for, was to feel normal... I guess be careful what you wish for. I awoke that morning to find my arm healed. I was the happiest I'd ever been in my whole life. For the first time, I felt like I looked like everyone else.' She coughs to clear her throat, Jordan hands her a bottle of water he was holding. She then smiles after taking a drink, points back to her brother, 'This is my little brother, and he had a disease that took his eyesight. I was so excited about my fortune, that I convinced him to touch the purple Orb also... And now he can see again. I was told by the Remaks that they picked me, I was someone special. I thought I was supposed to share what happened to me with everyone else, and I never asked why. My friends and I came up with a plan, to share with the world our good fortune. So far, we helped about 70 people, and within that, took

79

donations so we could help rebuild our suffering city. We just wanted to help, that's all." Rebecca's tears start rolling down her face, she looks back at Hope. Hope is crying too but smiles, and lips to her "Go on." Rebecca looks out into the crowd and sees her Uncle Ed. Rebecca says, "I'm sure you all saw my Uncle yesterday, condemning what we are doing here. Saying it was the work of the purple devil, it was unholy and that it would change you. My Uncle was right in one area of his statement. If you touch the Orb, some of the Remaks attach to you. But in doing so. If you have an ailment, you will be healed, if you have a disfigurement, it will be fixed, and if you have a sickness you will be cured. And your life expectancy will be double." The whole crowd gasps with "Cheers and Oh my God's and thank you Jesus's". Rebecca looks over the crowd and says precisely, "People, listen, if any of you touch this Orb, please know, you will not be 100% human, no more! This is the price you must pay." This time the crowd hears it and some cheers turn to jeers, boos and name-calling. A female reporter yells, "What do they look like?" Rebecca trying to answer over the chatter says, "They once looked like us, sort of, but they've evolved through time. They are now, forms of light energy. I don't know, to understand it more I'd tell you to touch the Orb. They can explain better than I can. But that would be at your own risk." Another reporter yells out, "Do they talk to you? She answers, "Yes, only through my dreams." The female reporter yells, "Did they come here to invade our planet?" Rebecca, unsure replies "I don't think so, but in a way, I guess so." The crowd sounds of an angry mob, chants of "Purple Devil start echoing within them. Beverly quickly grabs Rebecca and yells to her, "Go to the house now!" She looks at Damon and the football team, some have already left, she says, "Go home!" Rebecca looks at Beverly and says, "I'm not afraid of their opinion or their name-calling, I've been through this before. What I don't want this mob to scare off people, to persecute people that want to make this decision. We are here to help, and that's what we'll keep doing." Beverly winks at Rebecca and says, "I talked to the cops, they will arrest anyone that goes on the property they said. One of them brought in his mother a day ago with cancer. He's incredibly grateful." Rebecca smiles, her phone chimes, she looks and sees a message from her mom telling her, Uncle Pete will be there in ten minutes with the Governor. Rebecca says to her people, "Shit the governor will be here in ten minutes." The crowd of 80 plus people are loud, the pro and anti-sides yelling insults at each other with the cops in between. They take up the whole road in front of the house, traffic is at a standstill, as the chaos ensues. A man and his family push their way through the crowd. The man and woman are carrying a visibly sick 11yr girl. The dad says, "We drove here from Missouri, we are the Kinney's, my daughter Sarah is suffering from leukemia, please help us. Rebecca tells Beverly to guard the entrance, and she starts walking the couple back to the house. Just then Uncle Ed's bull horn starts playing its tune. Rebecca dismisses the noise, smiles at the family, and says, "Don't worry, we're gonna fix your daughter right up.

Inside the house, Hope is setting up for donations, she says to Rebecca as she walks in, "I'm not a lawyer, but we should probably start making people sign a waiver from now on." Rebecca says, "That's a good idea." Hope says, "It's crazy out there, you alright?" Rebecca says, "No, but I will be, we are gonna cure this little girl of her leukemia." Rebecca smiles looks at the little girl, and happily says, "Hi Sarah, my name is Rebecca, and this is Hope, we'll be helping you today. I must go over some important information before we can go ahead and kick that bad disease right out of your body. Okay?" Rebecca goes on to describe everything, and the parents sign the waiver at the end, along with a nice $300 donation. Just then, Professor Lambkin walks in the front door followed by Uncle Pete, the Governor, four of his staff members, and three security personnel. Uncle Pete says, "Where's Maggie?" Rebecca replies, "She's at work Uncle Pete." Pete frustrated says, "Excellent, she was supposed to be here by now." The governor looks Rebecca up and down and says, "My, haven't you grown up a lot since I saw you last." Rebecca replies, "Yes sir I have, and my arm is better too." He replies, "I know, Pete told me what happened on the way here. I'm so happy for you … and your brother too. If I may ask, do you have contact with these aliens?" Rebecca replies, "Yea, but only when I'm asleep, they're called Remaks. They are very friendly and say they're here to help us. They said we should be better to each other. Live in harmony or something like that. I don't know if humans would ever work like that, but my arms fixed, Jordan can see and this girl is about to be leukemia-free by tomorrow so that's a start, right? The governor doesn't know what to say and just nods his head. She continues, "I'm sure you're wondering what you have to do with this? Governor, we need your help, I hope after all you witness here today, you believe and will want to help us." The governor asks, "Can I see it?" Rebecca replies, "Well I'm taking this family to the barn to help this little girl right now. If the family doesn't mind, you can tag along with your people." They look to the family and they nod approval. Rebecca says, "Great then, let's go." As they walk through the kitchen Jordan waves at the governor, the governor returns the gesture in disbelief, the governor asks, "Professor Lambkin showed me a lab video of his blood fighting off diseases. This really, is all true?" Rebecca chuckles and says, "Yes. Prepare to be amazed!"

Rebecca leads everyone outside towards the barn. Heckling from Uncle Ed, his few followers and reporters shouting questions, fill the summer air. Rebecca says to the governor, "Sir, we need protection." He says, "Why don't you hire security then?" She replies, "No, not from them, we need protection from the United States government." The governor looks at Rebecca bewildered. They enter the barn and he sees the Orb, with its tempting mysticism and he says, "Oh, I see why you would you need protection from the United States government?" Rebecca says, "Never forget what you see here." He replies, "Oh I'm sure I won't." Rebecca turns her attention to the little girl, she makes her feel comfortable, then helps her touch the Orb. The governor watches, and he's intrigued by what he sees. All his staff have their phones out, recording the miracle from the stars in progress. Rebecca then tells the parents the girl's after-care and they exit the barn. Rebecca explains to the Governor, "What you just saw was the initial phase, the girl will now go sleep and when she wakes up, her body will be reborn…voila!" The governor says, "This all sounds too good to be true. There's gotta be a catch." Rebecca somberly says, "Yes, there is one. A little part of the Remaks is added to you, forever. Their existence becomes part of yours. The tradeoff is that you become smarter, stronger, immune to disease, and longer life… I was a little angry at first because I didn't quite understand. But after seeing all that has been achieved, it seems like a win-win situation, I'll take it." She looks at everyone gathered in the barn and says, "The F.B.I. wants to take this away from us, I just know they'll militarize this somehow, and ruin all the good that can come for it.' She refocuses on the governor, 'But if you stop them, you can save Michigan. People will come from all over the world for this, I know it. They will donate to help rebuild Flint and even all of Michigan." She grabs the governor's hand and continues, "I can see it, it will happen, but we need your help." Amidst the noise, Rebecca hears someone shouting, she looks towards the road and sees Beverly running towards the barn screaming, "They're back! They're back!" Rebecca looks to the road and sees four black F.B.I. Suburbans driving onto the property. Rebecca quickly says to the governor, "I need you to touch the Orb." Astonished he says, "What?!" She replies, "You need to see this for yourself..., please?" The governors' team quickly grab the governor to take him away, hastily he fights free and leaps for the Orb. He's laying outreached flat on his stomach as he's touching the Orb. He breaks contact after a few moments' rolls on his back laughing and screaming in delight. His team picks him off the ground like a baby, and he looks at Rebecca and says, "That's amazing oh my god, one of the greatest feelings I've ever had in my life. Holy shit. Does that happen every time you touch it?" Rebecca hurriedly says, "No, governor you need to go now. You'll fall asleep real soon, when you wake up though, you'll be superhuman. Use your powers and help us." The governor says, "You're family, you need only ask once." He winks at her as his team whisks him away to his car. Beverly runs up with her bat, breathing heavily says, "They said they have a warrant. They're gonna take you away!!" Pete and Professor Lambkin have been watching everything unfold, in silence. Pete interjects commandingly, "Close and lock the barn doors now. Professor and you girls get out of here, I'll stay and hold the door. We can't let them take the Orb or anyone." Professor Lambkin says, "I'm stronger than I've ever been in my life, I'm not going anywhere. I'll stay and fight." A stalemate happens for a couple of seconds, then Rebecca says, "Beverly, take the professor I'll stay with my uncle." Beverly nods grabs the reluctant professor's hand, and pulls him out of the barn. Beverly throws the lock and chain to Rebecca's feet as she closes the main door. They keep eye contact till the doors are pinched closed. Right before it shuts, Beverly makes a silly evil grin and throws a kiss to Rebecca. Rebecca takes a deep breath and softly smiles as she loses sight of her friend. Uncle Pete helps Rebecca chain lock the door then barricades it with hay bales. They then go around covering up the side door and small holes on the walls, by stacking bales. When they are done, the pulsing Orb is emitting the only light they have to see. Its pulse coincides with Rebecca's racing heartbeat. Rebecca stands over the Orb, closes her eyes and concentrates, her Uncle Pete looks on in amazement. The Orb's pulse stops then turns on bright, lighting up the barn. Pete says, "How did you do that?" Rebecca smiles and winks, then reply, "It's a kind of magic." The duo runs around checking for breach spots and fortify them as much as possible. After they're done inspecting their work, Uncle Pete says, "Don't worry kiddo, I won't let them take you." Rebecca says, "I know Uncle."

Things do not improve. Mr. Jenkins broadcasts over a loudspeaker, "Put down the bat and move away from the barn, we don't want to hurt you Beverly." They hear Beverly shout back "I don't want to hurt you either. So why don't you and you F.B.I. homeboys, go back where you came from." The outside banter continues, Rebecca says to Uncle Pete, "I need to do something, you need to not let anyone in here...I'll be back." Uncle Pete says, "I got you." Rebecca runs to the Orb slides across on her knees and makes contact. She opens her eyes to the Remak's figure standing in front of her. She excitedly says, "I need you to go, get in the Orb and get out of here, they're coming to take you!" The Remaks reply, "You need only think of a place and the Orb will transport itself there, Rebecca." Their conversation is suddenly interrupted, by the deafening sounds of Bang! Bang! Bang! Rebecca is being shook, she hears, "Wake up Rebecca, Rebecca wake up!" Uncle Pete yells, "They shot Beverly." Rebecca gets up and runs to the door and shouts out, "Jenkins tell me you didn't. Tell me you did not just shoot my friend?" There's quiet for a moment then Jenkins replies, "I gave her all the opportunity in the world, to give up Rebecca, she chose to challenge us, she chose that, and she lost. What do you want to do now? You can come out and give up, let us have the Orb and we'll leave you, never to return." Rebecca screams out, "You asshole Jenkins, you're a liar, you'd never leave us alone...

You're gonna pay for shooting my friend, you'll never get the Orb, you hear me. Never!" Rebecca goes to her uncle and says, "Uncle the Orb needs to leave now! I need you to think of a specific place when you touch the Orb and it'll go there." Uncle Pete says, "Why can't you?" She says, "Because you've been to more places, and I may slip up and tell them when they interrogate me. They don't want you they want me. Think of somewhere safe and far away. We can go get it later. Hurry up Uncle, you need to send the Orb away now!" Uncle Pete in a panic rolls his eyes trying to think of a place, then it hits him, he blurts out, "I've got one!" Suddenly a projectile burst through the wall, into the barn then explodes, releasing tear gas into the air. Then two more come crashing in. The last canister explodes, igniting some loose hay, which quickly starts spreading throughout the barn. Pete startled by this, hears Rebecca yell, "Touch it, touch it now!" Pete's hand waivers over the top of the Orb, he closes his eyes envisioning the location, then touches the Orb, which instantly glows bright emerald green. Pete gets thrown back twenty feet towards the back of the barn. The ground and barn begin to rumble, like being hit with an earthquake... The Orb emits a giant green flash, and then bursts out of the top of the barn leaving a string trail of smoke, in its wake. The barn is now enveloped by toxic gas and smoke from the canisters, the fire has spread fast, engulfing the walls and ceiling, feeding on everything in its path... It's like Hades. Rebecca attempts to run to her uncle when a truss collapses between them. It brings down an abundance of fiery debris with it, making extracting her uncle hopeless. Uncle Pete hunched over scurries his way through, barring his face to avoid the smoke and gas, but the debris and fire are too intense, he is trapped. Then there's a loud crash, as the front doors are rammed open by the F.B.I. A team of six come rushing in, to evacuate Rebecca and Pete. The team sees Pete surrounded by flames, he nods to them, then yells out to Rebecca, "PAM... PAM!!" They grab Rebecca, it takes all six men to pull her out as she resists. She never breaks eye contact with her uncle, she screams, "No Uncle Pete, No, Please save my Uncle Pete, Uncle Pete No... Somebody save my Uncle Pete." The team drags her out to a safe distance, where she shakes them off of her, to watch the inferno in peace. Maggie and Ed storm the agents, as they attempt to save their brother. Ed is being restrained by two agents, and it takes five agents to finally subdue Maggie who has injured four agents in the tussle. Everyone goes silent, they hear the screams of her Uncle Pete being burned alive. There's a loud snap of a supporting beam, then the barn crumbles upon itself in a thunderous roar. Rebecca, Maggie, and Ed all fall to their knees in shock. Rebecca is crying, she takes a breath to bawl but nothing but silence is heard. She then takes a second breath and releases it in a fit of rage, she bellows out a shriek so deafening it brings everyone to their knees, holding their ears in sheer pain. Maggie breaks free of her restrainers and runs to her daughter. She embraces Rebecca and they both sob inconsolably. Ed holding his ears with a blank look on his face looks at the two women weeping, gets up in dire shock, and aimlessly starts walking away. Rebecca with tears in her eyes says, "Mom Uncle Pete is dead, and I couldn't save him, they killed him. They killed Beverly too." She turns and looks for Mr. Jenkins, points, and yells, "He killed them!" Rebecca lets go of her mother and makes a beeline for Jenkins. Four of his men make a feeble attempt to try and stop her, but it's to no avail, all of them are still in too much pain from the shriek, one by one they easily get tossed aside like ragdolls. She makes it to Jenkins and picks him off the ground against the side of a suburban. She screams "Murderer!" Jenkins quickly says in a panic, "Beverly's not dead, she was shot with rubber bullets. She's being tended to right now in the ambulance right over there.' He points at the medical team attending to Beverly by the roadside. Rebecca drops Jenkins and runs over to the gurney where Beverly lies down. She is conscious with bandages wrapped around her chest area. Beverly somberly says, "I'm okay, doesn't hurt a bit." She gets up from the gurney and hugs Rebecca. She says, "I'm so sorry, I couldn't stop them." Rebecca sadly says, "My Uncle Pete's dead. I froze up, maybe I could have helped him, I was afraid. I'm no hero, I'm not, what they thought." Beverly tries to ease her pain and says, "Honey, there's nothing you could have done." Rebecca looks at her in her eyes and says, "Is there…?" Rebecca hears rustling behind her, its Jenkin's men guns raised, cautiously encroaching around her. She says with her back turned, "You just don't know when to quit, do you?" Rebecca goes to retaliate, and Beverly stops her saying, "I can't believe I'm saying this, but don't. Just go with them and come back.

Don't do this in front of your mother and brother." Rebecca looks over and sees her mom holding Jordan as he's rocking back and forth, traumatized. There are tons of onlookers everywhere, their property looks like a zoo of people. Rebecca turns around to Jenkins and in a serious tone says, "I'm ready to go with you now, but I can't promise I won't kill you." She then sternly says to Beverly, "Get all these damn people out of here and off my property. The Orb is gone, the shop is closed. Tell them to leave my family in peace. Nice Rebecca is no more."

chapter ten

P.A.M.

Agent Jenkins sat in the backseat with Rebecca for the hour-long trip back to F.B.I main building in Lansing. There was an uncomfortable silence on the drive. Every attempt of communication by Jenkins is met with looks of condemnation. She just sits, staring out of the window, occasionally wiping away a tear. They reach the building at 3:23 pm, there are countless reporters huddled around the front door. Agent Jenkins detours and drives to the back entrance within the gated area. In the building, Rebecca is led down through a hallway into the main office where agents are working. Every one of them stops what they are doing to get a glimpse of the alien surrogate. She is put into an interview room and told Agent Jenkins will be with her shortly. Twenty minutes go by before a female agent enters. She closes the door and sits down across the table from Rebecca, who is just looking down at the table. She sighs and says, "Hello Ms. Marshall, I'm Agent Summers, I am sorry for your loss. We heard about your uncle. Rebecca drearily says without looking up, "Where's Agent Jenkins?" The agent replies, "We thought it would be better if you didn't have any more contact with him, given your history." Rebecca replies, "I'll only talk to him, no one else." Agent Summer sits back in her chair and says, "Okay..." She then gets up and exits the room, moments later Agent Jenkins enters and sits down. After three minutes of no words, Agent says, "I am sorry about your uncle."

Rebecca emotionlessly replies, "What do you want?" He scoots his chair up to her and says, "Rebecca, you have really caused a frenzy here. Everyone from doctors to the president of the United States is calling us wanting to know if there's a miracle cure, or are we being invaded by aliens. We have a nation in unrest because of you. You need to tell me everything that has happened in the last few days and where the thing that shot out of your barn went to. Right here, right now." At this point, Rebecca is emotionally drained and empty. She feels like maybe the burden of this whole ordeal can be over, maybe if she tells them what they want to hear, she can go home and just be a normal kid again. She looks up and is about to tell them when there's a knock on the door. Agent Summers opens the door and says to Jenkins, "Her lawyers here." As the door fully opens Rebecca sees a well-built tall middle-aged man in a nice-looking suit, in a deep voice says, "Hello I am Mr. Pendleton, I've been retained to represent you, Ms. Marshall." He looks at Jenkins and says, "I've looked over your warrant and there's nothing in there towards detaining my client. It only pertained to the Orb and since that's no longer in my client's possession, this conversation is over." Mr. Pendleton assists Rebecca to her feet and escorts her out. Just then, a supervisor walks up to Jenkins and says, "Excuse me, Agent Jenkins, I just got off the phone with headquarters. I'm afraid you've been put on administrational leave till further notice." Agent Jenkins gasps, "What!? Why?" The supervisor replies, "Headquarters is getting a lot of calls concerning the way you conducted the warrant on the Marshall property. The live nationwide broadcast death of Peter Marshall was not good for the department. They want your full report ASAP. I also need you to please turn in your badge and duty weapon while your suspension is under investigation." Agent Jenkins in disbelief hands over his gear and slumps down into a chair. Rebecca stops in front of him and somberly says, "My Uncle Pete was an amazing man, you took him away from me. Sucks when a person just shows up and ruins your life, by taking away something you care about, huh?" She then turns and walks out with the lawyer. As they walk down the hallway Rebecca softly asks, "Who hired you?" He replies, "Sorry Ms. I'm not at the liberty to disclose that at this time. I have a car waiting for you to take you home. Powerless to challenge the man in the nice suit,

Agent Jenkins complies and releases Rebecca. On their way out of the building, the lawyer takes off his suit jacket and covers Rebecca's head. There's still a lot of eager reporters waiting outside, who now are accompanied by pro and con supporters. Mr. Pendleton looks at her smiles and says, "Okay take my hand, I'm going to lead you through the crowd the car is just on the other side." Rebecca nods and says. "Okay…I'm ready." The two make a steady dash towards the awaiting car. There's yelling of all types, questions from reports and obscenities, and name-calling from the protesters. For the moment, Mr. Pendleton trades in his license to practice law to become a bodyguard, Rebecca feels like she's in the movie. They finally get to the car, it's a stretched Cadillac. Rebecca had never been in a car this luxurious and she's curious as to who would send it. Once safely inside. Mr. Pendleton calmly says to the driver, "Get us out of here." The Cadillac speeds away from the crazed crowd, Rebecca softly says, "There's a lot of people that hate me… I don't understand." Mr. Pendleton reaches for a water bottle out of the ice bucket, cracks it open, and hands it to Rebecca, "I don't hate you, and neither does the person that hired me. I just cannot tell you who it is at this time." Rebecca takes the water and sadly smiles looks out the window and says, "I just want to go home." She takes out her phone and texts her mom she's coming home. Then snuggles up against the car door and stares as the city goes by.

The Cadillac arrives back at the Marshall's resident just about sunset. The crowds of people have disappeared leaving only their litter as a remembrance. Maggie walks out of the house as the car drives up the driveway. Rebecca jumps out as soon as the car stops and runs to embrace her mother. The lawyer gets out and introduces himself to Maggie. He hands her two business cards, one his personal, and tells her to call him if there's ever a need. He then tells her to please call the number that's on the second card. He then consolable says, "It's a pleasure to have met you both and I'm sorry for your loss." Mr. Pendleton then gets in the car and drives off. Maggie looks at the second card and there's only a number written on it. Rebecca stares at the mountain of smoldering rumble that was once their barn. She can see the charred skeleton of Caroline under some debris. Maggie consolingly says, "They found your uncle and took him away about an hour ago." Rebecca starts crying and says, "I can't believe he's gone." Maggie holds her daughter tight and walks her into the house.

In the house, the laughter and busyness of the past few days have been replaced with decimating sadness. In the center of the dining table stands a picture of Uncle Pete, with a candle burning next to it. The picture shows him sitting on the edge of a cliff looking at a mountain valley. It was Maggie's favorite picture of her brother. Uncle Ed had found his way back and sat motionless staring at muted Sports Center, tears running down his face. He looks like he's aged ten years in the day. Maggie softly brushes his shoulder with her hand as she walks past him to the kitchen. Jordan is sitting at the kitchen table, dazed he smiles at Rebecca as she sits down next to him and he solemnly says, "I'm glad you're back home, I thought I'd never see you again." Rebecca replies, "I'm glad I'm home too." Maggie sets down the two business cards on the kitchen table as she goes to prepare some hot chocolate for her children and Ed. Jordan says, "What's this?" Rebecca replies, "Some lawyer got me out of talking with the F.B.I. and drove me home. He left us his number and this other number to call. Mom, are you going to call it? It could be the person who hired him. If so, I'd like to at least thank him." Maggie says, "These last few days I've been getting calls from all over, either wanting to give or take something. I don't have the energy to talk to anyone right now. You want to reach out and touch someone, go ahead be my guest, it's literally your call." Rebecca takes out her phone and sees Hope and Beverly have texted her, wanting to know how she's doing. She replies and tells them she's home and loves them. She then gives the card to her brother and tells him to read out the number. As he's reading it out, the area code seems foreign to her. The phone starts ringing…and ringing. Rebecca is about to hang up when she hears a male voice say, "Hello." Rebecca says, "Hello, hi my name is Rebecca, did you hire a man named Mr. Pendleton to be my lawyer?" The man says, "Yes, I did, were you satisfied with him?" She replies, "Yes, he was nice, thank you for sending him." Confused she asks, "Who are you?" He replies, "My name is Trevor Washington. I'm your father." Rebecca stunned by what she heard, hangs up on him. Maggie serves her two kids their hot beverage, then grabs the one she made for Ed and asks,

"So who was it, some rich fat cat wanting privileges with the Orb?
Rebecca softly replies, "He said he was my father." A loud smash is
heard, Maggie is stopped dead in her tracks after dropping the mug.
The shattered mug pieces are all over the floor along with the hot
chocolate. Maggie says in shock, "Did he say his name was Trevor
Washington?" Rebecca nods her head. Maggie sternly says, "Call
him back, and put it on speaker." The phone rings and as soon as
Trevor answers Maggie lays into him. "You really have some nerve
contacting us after all these years. You asshole! You have no idea
about the day that Rebecca's had and for you drop fuckin Star Wars,
I am your father bullshit. That has got to be, just the worst timing
announcement ever. You wanted to be out of our life 18yrs ago,
you should have stayed gone. Why the hell are you reaching out to
us now anyway? You want something right?" Trevor calmly replies,
"No, not at all. I can't begin to apologize for the last 18 years. I only
found out about Rebecca a few days ago." Maggie interrupts, "You
liar!! I told you I was pregnant with your baby." Trevor continues, "I
know you did. Then shortly thereafter a young man came up to me
and told me that he was the father, you were seeing him for years.
That I was just being played for my money. I was young and stupid,
I was heartbroken and believed him and so I left and went back to
my family in Hawaii." Maggie in shock says, "What? Who told you
they were with me? That is a lie, you took my virginity, Trevor. I
had never been with another man but you." Trevor replies, "I know
that's true now. I am so sorry. My mother passed away last week,
she admitted to me on her death bed, that she paid someone to tell
me that. She was very racist at the time and didn't want to see me
with a black woman. She was ashamed of what she did and did not
want to die without bearing the truth to me. When I found out I
immediately research you and saw that Rebecca had graduated. I
was planning on having a better introduction but after seeing her
get arrested on the news I figured I'd intervene and help if possible.
I'm sorry if I overreached, I just wanted to help, and that's all. I am
terribly sorry about your loss today. Please know, I may not have been
there all these years, but I'm here now. I want to be a part of your
lives, in any way possible. I hired Mr. Pendleton for you, he's the best.
If law enforcement or government agency harasses you call him. I'll

go now and let you grieve in peace. If either of you has any questions or just want to talk, please don't hesitate to call day or night. Maggie, I'm sorry again. Good night." Trevor hangs up, Maggie is looking out of the back window above the sink, and she turns around with tears rolling down her face. She bends down to clean up the mug and spilled beverage and says to herself, "Racist Bitch." Rebecca goes to help and she says, "Becca stop, go drink your cacao, I'll clean this up." There's a silence at the table again, Jordan trying to ease his sister's feelings says, "He sounds rich, you can tell him to start with, all the back birthday and Christmas gifts. Rebecca smiles at her brother for his effort then says, "I see you." She then gets up and says, "Mom, I think I'm going to go to bed." Maggie stops cleaning, stands up, and says, "You wanna sleep in my bed tonight?" Rebecca says, "I'd like that, thanks, mom." Maggie replies, "I'll be in, in a little bit." Mentally exhausted, Rebecca heads off to her mother's room to try and sleep away the events that had transpired. It's not every day you lose an uncle and gained a father.

Rebecca's tired body falls into a deep sleep only a few minutes after she lays down. As usual, she awakens sitting on the hilltop cliff overlooking the ocean. The Remaks appeared and take a seat next to her. Her guilt overwhelms her heart, she feels responsible for her uncle's death. She asks, "Why did he have to die? Why couldn't it have been me instead? Can't you do something, can't you bring him back?" The beings reply, "We are so sorry you lost your uncle Rebecca, we can feel your pain. We have not felt this since our people were lost. But, just like we could not have brought our people back, we cannot bring your uncle back. None of the civilizations we have visited have that power. The rule is once a light force is ignited, it can be prolonged by the invention but once it is extinguished, it is no more." Rebecca says, "What about you guys? How come you can live so long? The being answers, "We can die, we only learned how to transfer our energy." She snidely replies, "So now you live in all of us then, you cheated death by using us." The being replies, "No, only you. We are alive only in you. Our biological imprint was added to the people you helped, not our life force. They still have free will over their thoughts and decisions. They are still bound to the natural order. You, however, carry our life blood, when you die, we will also."

Rebecca remorseful of her crassness look at the being kindly then reaches out to hold its hand. The being's hand looks like a fingerless mitten, and it is much larger than hers. The being looks at the gesture and it is welcomed. She then says, "Let's not talk about death, and just sit here with me for a while." The being says, "As you wish." She smiles. That night Rebecca slept harder than she had ever slept before. She woke up around 1 am and saw her mother was not in the bed with her. She gets up and searches the house, her uncle was in one of the bedrooms sleeping and her brother was also in his room. Concerned, she then goes out on the front porch and looks over the property. That is when she sees her mother in the open field sitting on a chair by the barn rumble. Rebecca quietly walks over to her mother, she can hear faint whimpering as she gets closer. She sees smoke rising off long ash of a lit cigarette in her hand. With tears rolling down her face Maggie softly says, "July is just not a good month for the Marshalls." Rebecca reaches for Maggie's hand, stands her up, and then she walks her loving mother to her bed, tucking her in and kissing her on the forehead. Rebecca goes to her room and stares at the circling ceiling fan. Thousands of thoughts run through her mind from her father to Agent Jenkins. She ponders everything racing in her head till she falls back to sleep.

When daybreak came Ed was the first to awake. He wrote a note and left it on the dining table. Jordan was second to wake up, he made himself some cereal and took it into his room. Rebecca woke up and group texted Hope and Beverly, "Good Morning, thank you for everything I love you, girls." Hope texted back, "Love you too Becca do you want me to come over." Rebecca texts, "No, I'm gonna look after my mom today make sure she's ok." Hope texts back, "Okay, lemme know if you need anything." Beverly then adds, "Same goes for me." Rebecca then gets up and goes to check on her mom, she sees she's asleep still then checks on everyone else in the house. Jordan has gone back to bed. She sees the note Ed left, it reads "I hope you all can forgive me for my selfish actions, I am ashamed, and I'm lost without my brother. I'll be at the church if you so choose to ever want to see me." Rebecca still had not spoken to her uncle since this all happened. She thought maybe this would be an opportunity to clear the air with her elder. She made herself a piece of toast, then got ready to take a walk to her uncle's church.

It was a quiet Thursday morning as Rebecca walked out her front door. Her Uncle Pete's truck was still parked by the house, she got the shivers as she walked past it, brushing her fingers down the side of it. The heavy smell of smoke from the burnt debris still filled the air. She walked faster down the road till it dissipated and was replaced with the natural scent of country trees. The roads were empty compared to the past few days. A sense of calm blanketed everything she saw. The neighbor's dogs were not barking up a storm like normal when she walked by. The birds' chirping wasn't echoing from tree to tree like normal, even the wind has seemed to stand still. Rebecca felt like nature was having its own moment of silence for her Uncle Pete. She knew it was all a coincidence, but all the same, it comforted her.

Walking up to the church made Rebecca feel weird. She wasn't overly religious, to begin with. Growing up she always had more questions than the Sunday school teacher, Miss Sampson could give answers to. She had spent many of her Sundays in the corner asking what Miss Sampson considered obscure questions. With all she'd experience in the last few days she's sure Miss Sampson was rolling in her grave. As she entered the doors, she smelled the heavenly air of an old wooden church glazed in linseed oil. It was built in the 1930s during the Sit-Down Strike, originally a Protestant church. After automotive plant closures, it was abandoned in 1979. In 1991 Ed purchased the property and with the help of family and neighbors restored the house of God, naming it Fellowship Church. It held around 100 people on comfortable pews, along with a donated electric organ that Mrs. Sarah would religiously lead parishioners in song every given Sunday. It was a quant place that Ed built as his legacy.

Rebecca looks for her uncle who said he'd be in the church but was nowhere to be found in the church. She heads outside to the back towards the little house Ed lived in. Rebecca then sees her uncle digging by himself next to her grandparent's burial plots. He notices her as she walks up but continues with his chore. He says, "Is it just you?" She replies, "Yea, mom, and Jordan are still sleeping." He stops digging briefly then says, "You must hate me or at least blame me for Peter's death." Rebecca replies, "I don't hate you Uncle, I did feel like you hated me. All those things you said hurt." Ed stops then walks up to Rebecca and says, "Child I could never hate you. You are my sister's child, the heiress to the Marshall name. I apologize for my ill-mannered actions. It was impetuous, rooted in jealousy and ignorance. My brother was always the more levelheaded one of us both. He explained, but I didn't want to listen. Now he's gone and am burdened with guilt. When he dropped me off two nights ago, I told him that this was an abomination and anyone taking part in it would be met with the lord's wrath. I did not think that would be my last words to him. Now my brother is dead." Ed slumps down and Rebecca sees him realize the words he just said. The strong man everyone is used to breaks, he begins bawling uncontrollably which is contagious, Rebecca starts also. They embrace each other and grieve for their lost loved ones. Ten minutes go by and slowly the weeping subsides. Ed takes Rebecca into his house and gives her bottled water. He then goes on to tell her stories of him and Pete growing up. This goes on for a half-hour then there's a moment of silence, Rebecca asks, "Are you digging Uncle Pete's grave?" Ed replies, "Yes, would you like to help?" Rebecca eagerly replies, "Uncle, I would be honored." Ed gets her a shovel and they resume digging. Ed shares even more stories with Rebecca. This is the first time she has spent this much time with her uncle, and she begins to feel a bond growing. It takes them about 4 ½ hours to dig the grave, they get done around 2:30 pm. Rebecca's phone rings, she checks it and sees it's her mom calling. She answers, "Hi mom, you okay?" Maggie responds, "I texted you twice, where are you?" Rebecca replies, "Oh sorry, I'm with Uncle Ed, we just dug Uncle Pete's grave." Maggie says, "Did Ed put him next to mom and dad?" Rebecca says, "Yes." She replies, "Tell him we'll need more flowers, and we'll set the funeral for July 10th same as mom and dad." Rebecca replies, "That's what he was thinking also." Maggie says, "Okay, tell him I want him to come for dinner." Rebecca replies, "Okay mom I'll tell him, I'll be home soon. Love you, Bye." Rebecca hangs up with her mother then goes inside the house where Ed is. He's washing his hands and face in the kitchen sink. He grabs a towel off the fridge door handle and says, "I'm sorry for what I put you through Rebecca. I don't know what you have in you, but if you say they chose you... Then I believe god made you for them, to represent us. I don't think they could have picked a better person... And who am I to argue with the almighty." He smiles at his niece and then says, "All this digging made me hungry, how about I drive us down to Famous Dave's for some BBQ?" Rebecca happily replies, "Hell yea, oh I mean, yeah I'd love that." Ed replies, "Good then I'll drop you home." Rebecca interjects, "Mom wants you over for dinner." Ed takes a second then says, "Well you know there's no saying no to your mother. So okay." Rebecca cleans herself up and they both get in Uncle Ed's 1999 Ford Ranger and they head off to eat.

From the moment Rebecca entered the restaurant she could feel eyes on her. From young to old people had their phones out to get a caption. Ed saw this and puffed up his chest to try and ward off any advancements. They ordered their food-to-go and left. Ed drove to a quiet spot he knew close by, with a great view of the Flint River. Rebecca thanked her uncle for seeing she was uncomfortable, he winked at her as he emptied the bbq bag of treats. Ed and Rebecca both shared stories it was a moment she found precious reminiscing they laughed and cried over the shared meal.

It was 4:40 pm when Ed drove up the driveway to the house. He parks next to his brothers' truck, gets out, and slowly gazes over to the barn area as he walks into the house. The house smells of fresh bread and beef stew. Maggie's busy slaving away in the kitchen, a site a little unfamiliar these days, Rebecca asks, "What's wrong with Jordan?" Maggie proudly replies, "What do you mean, what's wrong with Jordan? He's a teenage boy, he don't need to be tied up in this kitchen all day. Plus, even he, with all his talent, can't make Uncle Pete's favorite dish like me." Rebecca watches her mother move about the kitchen, deep inside, she knows that Maggie is trying to keep herself occupied, to escape reality however she can. Ed sits down at the kitchen table and Maggie says, "Rebecca go get the bottle of scotch in the living room cupboard and pour me and your uncle a glass." Rebecca does as her mother asks, then comes back into the kitchen and is making the drinks as Maggie is talking to her brother. "Has anyone called you yet? My phone has been ringing nonstop." Ed replies, "I don't know. I left my phone in my bedroom all day. I'm normally the one handing out condolences, I wasn't ready to be on the receiving end today, again." Maggie takes her glass of 12yr old scotch and cheers her brother in honor of Pete. Maggie then says, "I already arranged the headstone I hope you don't mind. The whole family is coming for the funeral so the church might be a little full. If you want, we can just do it all outside, rain or shine." Ed somberly says, "That is fine. Maggie, I am…" Maggie instantly cuts him off, "Don't say a thing. You didn't kill Pete the asshole F.B.I. did. I just hope you apologized to your niece for what you put her through." Rebecca jumps in, "He did mom, and we had a good day together where he told me so many stories of him and Uncle Pete and you growing up." Maggie turns around and goes back to cooking and says, "Good." It becomes quiet for a few moments Rebecca can feel that Maggie has some pent-up resentment toward Ed, and so can Ed. Rebecca tries to change the subject by saying to her mom, "When do you think I should call my dad again?" Maggie chuckles and says, "Darling he's your father, you can call him anytime just don't mention me." Rebecca thinks, shit that's not a good topic either. Hoping to play on the fond memory heartstrings she says, "Uncle please tell me some more stories about you all growing up." The thing about Uncle Ed being a preacher is that he could tell a story in a way like you felt you were there living it, it was his gift. Ed proceeds to tell a story of all three kids growing up and tensions slowly relaxed. Maggie from time to time would let out a laugh, even Jordan came out of the room to listen. Dinner happened with just the four of them listening and telling stories about the dearly departed. The Marshall's were mourning yet again, and again it wouldn't be the last time.

The day of the funeral finally arrived. In the past week, Uncle Ed did his best to make amends with his family. Maggie trying to maintain and move forward from her brother's death brought home a one-year old golden retriever from the shelter. The kids had never had a dog as she did, she figured this would be a welcomed distraction to the on goings. Rebecca and Jordan picked up from years past, and each day they would take "Buddy", the name Jordan came up with, for a walk up to the hilltops. That's where Jordan realized his eyesight was a lot more than normal. He could see birds in trees a mile away, another bonus to the Remaks gift. Some evenings Hope and Beverly would join them on their adventure. Buddy running like a spaz all over, had enough energy to keep everyone entertained. And at night he would shuffle between the kids's rooms sleeping with each of them. Occasionally, people would stop by, wanting a miracle or a reporter looking for a story. The family would just call the local cop they knew and he would send a car over immediately to discourage the unwanted individuals. Rebecca still had her nightly meetings with her mental companions and both shared ideas and experiences. Trying their best to find a way to solve the world's problems. Everything seemed like maybe life would just go on, they would bury Uncle Pete and that would be the end of it. But it was only just the beginning, and deep inside, Rebecca knew this charade could not last too much longer.

The morning of the funeral Jordan got up extra early and made breakfast. Ham, eggs, and toast with hash browns were served. The funeral is at noon, Ed, Maggie, and some family members that came down set up all the chairs and tables the day prior. The Marshall family was not exceptionally large, mostly cousins, uncles and aunts which totaled maybe 50 people. Plus, neighbors they expected was about 30 tops, so this funeral was not going to be too extravagant. Rebecca and Jordan was told to be ready by 10:30am sharp, and they were. They both had brand new clothes for the occasion, Maggie wanted all of them to look the best for their uncle. Maggie finished getting ready and came out of her room in a beautiful black dress accented with a green handkerchief, her brother's favorite color. Rebecca and Jordan were also dressed in black with said kerchief. They see their mother and smile, Maggie fights back the tears as she adjust Jordan's tie. Maggie takes a deep breath and says, "Okay let's go…" They pack into the car, even Buddy, and head off to meet Uncle Ed who's at the church.

The weather this July 10th is quite pleasant, there are a few clouds in the sky but nothing threatening. The car is silent on the ride to the church, all except for Buddy's heavy panting. Maggie starts humming a strange song that's foreign to Rebecca, but it's soothing and makes the drive easier. As the family drives into the church parking lot, it is unexpectedly crowded. The parking lot is full. Maggie drives around in search of a spot to no avail. She then sees a cousin of hers running out from back waving her in. When he reaches her, he says, "Ed says

I needed to direct you to park in the back next to his house." As they drive back they see a sea of people unfamiliar to them all. Once out of the car Ed greets them and says, "People I don't know have been showing up to pay their respects from all over, and I mean from all over the world. There's a man that's never met Pete or our family here from Germany. He said he saw Pete's heroics on the television and was compelled to come. He said Rebecca is a gift and we must all support her and her family." Rebecca stops and says, "Wait, all these people are here because of me?" Ed says, "I'm afraid so, even our cousin Joshua the governor's here." Rebecca's big eyed and overwhelmed as the ocean of people part to make way for them, like Moses and the Red Sea. Uncle Ed takes Buddy and puts him out of the way in his house. They are directed down the walkway to the front of the ceremony. Maggie, Rebecca, and Jordan are guided through, all while the guest lathers them with condolences and gratitude. Finally, they are seated and then a line begins to form towards them. People are now handing envelopes to Maggie with well wishes and contributions to a new barn. Uncle Ed interrupts the crowd telling them the ceremony is about to commence. People take a seat where they can, the majority are standing all around the burial site focused on Uncle Ed by the casket. He starts by thanking everyone for coming and says how much the Marshall family appreciates it. Ed continues with his sermon to the crowd's vocal agreements of "Amen and Hallelujah." Rebecca hears none of it because she is still in shock at the number of people there, she is just staring at her uncle's tombstone that reads.

"Here Lies

Peter Alexander Marshall

Loving Brother, Uncle, and Friend to all."

Rebecca reads it over and over until she's startled by her mother saying, "Are you going up to say something? Ed just asked for you to come up and say some words." Rebecca's heart starts beating out of her chest, she slowly gets up and takes her uncle's place center stage and nervously says, "Good afternoon everyone, thank you again for coming to pay respects to my Uncle Pete. I know he would really appreciate knowing he was so loved." She pauses then says, "I was with him in his last moments... I really haven't thought about it much until now. I guess I've been blocking it out... my Uncle Pete was a very brave man. He believed in me and he believed in what I found...or what found me." She says under her breath. "He died trying to stop tyrants from taking away something for themselves that was supposed to be given to all of us. When we saw that was inevitable, I had my uncle send it away to a place only he knew. He died with that secret. I miss my uncle and I would trade it all back to have him here instead... But my Uncle Pete would disagree with me. His sacrifice was about helping as many people as we can, it's what the Marshalls would do. And that's what I will continue to do in his memory with or without the orb. Thank you for coming." Rebecca returns to her seat and throughout the rest of the ceremony, she is zoned out. Constantly reliving the barn and her uncle.

With the funeral finally over the family gets home around 5:30 pm, everyone is physically and emotionally drained. Maggie goes to her room to decompress and maybe get a nap, she hadn't slept well since her brother died. Jordan went to escape in his video games. Hope thought she should be there for her best friend. The two sit slumped down on the living room couch, speechless. Rebecca breaks the silence after some time saying softly, "The barn fire has been replaying in my head since the funeral, with so much detail. I can't stop remembering it." Hope says, "Do you feel guilty?" Rebecca looks at her and replies, "Immensely! But that's not it. My uncle's last words to me were Pam. I don't know a Pam. Maybe he knew a Pam and that may be a clue to where he sent the orb or something. I don't know... I just wish I could have saved my uncle." The girls resume the silence. Rebecca sits starring at the copper nugget on the coffee table. She reaches and picks it up nonchalantly looking it over as she smiles a little remembering how much Uncle Pete treasured his rock. While looking it over she sees her uncles carved in initials P.A.M... Her face instantly looks surprised, she looks at Hope and says out loud, "Eureka!! I know where it is! I know where the orb is! He said PAM, that's his initials, he carved on the nugget. He must have known I'd look at it and figure it out." Hope wide-eyed says, "Guess we're going on a road trip." Rebecca confidently says, "Yeah! Let's go find the orb." The two girls jump off the couch and go spread the news to Maggie and Jordan. Maggie suggests they take her Uncle Pete's truck for the excursion. The girls lay in bed working up game plans as they plan to leave come morning. That night Rebecca relays their findings to the Remaks and they fill her dreams with tranquility resting her body for the long day ahead.

chapter eleven

MASS CITY

Maggie was already awake and making breakfast for everyone when the girls woke. She had the girls sit as she served them their plates. Rebecca noticed she was overly quiet as they all ate. Just as they were about done eating. Maggie takes a sip from her orange juice and softly says, "I met Michael Hooks at the funeral yesterday." She gets up from the table and puts her dishes in the sink and continues, "He walked up to me and Ed, and introduced himself, gave his condolences then apologized for all the pain he's caused. He said he's been coming to Ed's services for over a year but never had the courage to say anything. I told him I forgave him and then he offered any help we needed, if we wanted it from him, then left. I still don't know how to feel about him though." She says all this as she's washing the dishes. The girls are dumbfounded and just looking at her weird calmness. Rebecca curiously asks, "Mom, who's Michael Hooks?" Maggie unemotionally replies, "Oh he's the man that killed your grandparents. I think I'm going to go to work today. Here's a credit card to use on your trip, do not buy anything stupid with it. Only necessary purchases." Rebecca in shock replies, "Okay mom." Maggie then says, "Oh, and let me know where you are every step of the way and where you're staying. I love you, gotta go." She gives Rebecca a kiss and heads out of the house. The two girls stare at each other blindsided by the information just bestowed upon them. As the initial shock wears off, the girls clean up and get ready for their journey. They make sure Jordan is taken care of food-wise. Then they drive over to Hope's place so she can pack a bag. Within this time Beverly texts Rebecca to see how she's holding up and she is also invited to go on the expedition, which she accepts. The three girls get on the road around 9:30 am, it's almost an 8hr drive to Caledonia Mine. Rebecca is happy her girls are with her, she is going on an adventure like her Uncle Pete used to do, to retrieve an item her uncle connected with. In the back of her mind she feels this will keep her Uncle Pete a part of her forever.

For the first 2hrs of the journey, all they could talk about was the new news about the killer of George and Mary. Since Rebecca was driving, Hope and Beverly were busily on their phones trying to look up any information out there on the web about 62yr old Michael Hooks. He was released from prison in 2002 and was on parole for 2yrs. Mr. Hooks was not on Facebook, Instagram or Twitter. He worked at a nursing home as a caretaker. He lived in a big six-bedroom home inherited by him after his parents died. The home was an hour away from Uncle Ed's church. It looks like he was trying to make amends in any way he could for his past deed. After a while, they got bored of the topic and decided to stop and get something to eat. They stopped at the Taco Bell in Grayling, and Rebecca inform her mom via text where they were so she wouldn't worry. The girls decided to eat in the restaurant in order not to get a car fever. While eating they tried to figure out where they were going to spend the night. This decision was simple since the only lodging in Mass City was called Adventureland Motel…it all made perfect sense. As they ate, something caught Rebecca's eye, she says, "I don't want to be paranoid but there's a white pickup truck parked across the road with two gentlemen in it and I think there are looking at us." The girls all look and the truck drives off. Hope says, "With looks like mine I'll be offended if they don't look." The girls all laugh then Hope says, "Girl you were all over the news you're famous, a celebrity now. People are gonna look, get used to it." Beverly interrupts, "And you're not the only celebrity out of this." Beverly then shows the girls on her phone, it's a video of a woman on a talk show claiming that the aliens impregnated her with Christ's second coming baby. Hope then says, "Yep, here we go."

The girls resume the road trip taking I-75 up and over the Huron Bridge then a US-2 scenic drive along the shoreline of Lake Michigan. They stopped every few hours for a bathroom break and to check in with Maggie. Maggie told Rebecca to make sure she always had at least half a tank of gas. So, Rebecca would just fill up the tank at every gas station they stopped at. Hope was sitting in the front passenger seat and Beverly had the backseat to herself. On the drive the girls talked about school, boys, and future plans like normal girls, pretending the last few days never happened. There were lots of laughs and it was a healthy break for them, especially Rebecca. They finally reached The Adventureland Motel around 7 pm and checked in. The motel was one story and painted all white. It looked like a big house with lots of adjoining rooms and you parked directly in front of your door. The girls were all starving, the colorful, meaning bright purple-haired old lady at the front desk told them, "Go to O'Henry's Inn 5 miles down the road, BEST dinner in town." They then went to scope out their room, as they entered, the layout reminded Rebecca of a typical motel room from every action movie. She chuckled to herself and says, "Get comfy girls, this is home for a few days." There are two beds one full and one queen, Beverly takes the full by putting her backpack on it first. Hope and Rebecca shrug their shoulders, Rebecca says, "Eh, just like home." They freshen up a little and head out.

The girls arrive at O'Henry's and find that in this red brick home restaurant, its Italian buffet night, Rebecca was in heaven. While scarfing on their food like it was their first meal ever. A young teenage girl walks over to their table and says, "Hi sorry to bother you. You are the Fearsome Three right?" The girls' bewildered look at each other confused then Rebecca asks the girl, "Where did you get that name?" The girl says, "The internet, there are pics of you three everywhere." The girl show them pics of them at the house and funeral, even from the Taco Bell they stopped at earlier. The girl then says, "Yeah and you all have powers, you can heal." She points to Rebecca, "And you are the muscle." She looks at Beverly. "And you, we don't quite know your powers are." Hope interjects, "I have the power of mind control.'

Hope points at Rebecca and Beverly, 'I tell them what to do." All the girls laugh, and the teenager mindlessly laughs along. Then the girl asks for their autograph which they gladly give her. As the girl walks off Hope says, "I guess we all celebrities in this mutha." Beverly adds, "Well perfect, I brought along a little bottle to commemorate. It's at the back of the hotel." Rebecca says, "Well, what are we waiting for, let's get back and turn this night up." The girl pack up the leftovers for later and scurry out of O'Henry's waving at the girl as they leave.

It was dark as the girls drove into their Adventureland parking spot. They got out and Rebecca noticed that the same white truck parked five spots down. She didn't say anything to the others because she didn't want them freaking out, seeing that they were in such a good mood. The motel at capacity had 11 rooms and it was almost full if the vehicles parked. In the room, Beverly pulls out an unopened handle of Fireball. Out of the three Beverly was the most experienced drinker, Rebecca and Hope had been drunk once before when they were 16 at a house party. Drunk meaning, they had five beers then went skinny dipping in the neighbor's pool. Beverly hurries out the door to get ice, the other two refrigerate the leftovers and change into more comfortable sleeping attire. Beverly returns and does likewise. After a half-hour, they could no longer wait for the bottle to chill. They crack into it, Beverly brought three shot glasses and each was to be owned and used only with the other two. She pours out the first shot and then yells out, "To the Fearsome Three!!" They all laugh and drink, Hope instantly squirms but then is like, I like it pour some more. Rebecca isn't fazed at all and says, "Another." The girls continue this ritual, toasting everything from Uncle Pete to Remaks to Caroline the lawnmower. This went on till midnight, Hope was the first to falter, and they all stopped drinking at this point and just laying on their backs in bed. Hope's eyes closed and mumbling says, "Rebecca I love you, I've loved you since the fifth grade. I know you don't feel the same for me and that's okay. I just want to tell you I love you, Becca." Hope then sits up bends over Rebecca and kisses her on the lips lays back and passes out. Rebecca looks over at Beverly who is laughing uncontrollably. Rebecca says, "What was that?" Beverly replies, "You really didn't know? You can see it every time she looks at you." Rebecca in shock says, "I seriously never knew." Beverly says, "Well you know now. And on that note, I'm going to bed and hey, I love you too." Beverly blows her a kiss then rolls over. Rebecca is pretty drunk but still quite aware, she gets up to go turn off the light. After she does she peaks the blinds and sees a figure by the white truck smoking a cigarette. She confirms the doors are locked and goes back into the bed. Laying there she recalls what Hope said and she finds her hand and holds it whispering, "I love you too." Shortly she passes out also.

Sunday 8:00 am phone alarm sounded like a freight train to Hope, she yelled out, "Turn it off!!" Rebecca wasn't worse for wear she reaches over and turns off her phone. She checks her messages and sees a text from Quintin "Hi stopped at your house. Told me you're away. Hurry back." Rebecca smiles and texts him, "Back before you know it." Rebecca gets up and sees the bottle of Fireball ¾ empty and sighs in astonishment. She peeks out of the blinds again and the white truck is no longer there. Rebecca smiles she's relieved and her paranoia can subside. Twenty minutes later Rebecca is showered and dressed, Beverly follows behind and then Hope takes her turn. While Hope is showering Rebecca says to Beverly, "Please don't mention the love thing, hopefully, she doesn't even remember, I'll talk to her when we get home." Beverly agrees and mums the word. The girls decide to have breakfast at Adventureland because it was complementary, which turned out to be surprisingly delicious. During the meal of egg, hash browns and bacon, they each put their two cents in on where to start and the manner of a search pattern. Hope's key repeated input was, "I need more Potatoes!" over and over again, "I need more Potatoes!" she was still a little drunk. Ultimately, they agreed on finding the big sycamore tree 2 miles northwest of Caledonia mine first, then devise a search grid plan. While walking back to the room after breakfast, they noticed it had drizzled giving everything a fresh coat of shimmering wetness. The smell of fresh green grass and asphalt filled the air. As Hope passes their truck, she notices a pretty rainbow sheen from under their truck. She comments, "Ouuu, pretty rainbow colors." Rebecca texted her mom to tell her they might be out of range later, since they would be hiking in the forest and not to worry. She replied with, "Be careful, stay together and I know you will find it. Love you,

Becca." Rebecca smiled and replied, "We will love you too." The girls got all that they needed from the room did a group cheer, "Fearsome Three!!" And headed out psyched for their adventure. There was a market next door to the motel which they raided for water and snacks, each of them filling their backpack with goodies. Beverly sat in the big back seat and Hope took the co-pilot seat up front. The Caledonia Mine opened at 9 am and was only ten minutes away. It was 9:23 am as the girls drove out, starting their grand excursion. The plotted directions on the phone said to take M-26. It was a short drive with simple directions. The final turn was left onto Caledonia Rd which ended up at the mine. Rebecca noticed the truck's brakes felt a little soft as they made the turn. They had 1 ½ mile to go on a lonely but well-groomed flat landed road. About a quarter-mile in Rebecca notices a vehicle approaching at a high rate behind her, within no time its right up on her back bumper. Rebecca yells out, "Oh my god, it's the white truck!" The other girls turn around to see two middle-aged men yelling and pointing at them, in a lifted white truck much like the one they were in, barreling upon them. Hope screams out, "Floor it, Becca!!" Rebecca mashes the pedal down to try get away from the crazed lunatics. The man driving the white truck is a more experienced driver and he comes alongside Rebecca with their window down. The girls are frightened as they hear the men shouting, "Alien Demon Burn In Hell, Satan's Children Die!!" The two trucks are side by side down straight away going about 85mph. Hope yells out, "Brake!" Rebecca slams on the brakes but nothing happens, she keeps pumping with no response. They all hear the male passenger laugh and say, "No brakes! No brakes! You die today." The white truck then speeds up and swerves right clipping the front of Uncle Pete's truck. Rebecca loses control and the truck veers right off the road into the ditch which catapults the truck and it begins flipping end over end seven times before coming to rest in a field. The truck is laying on its roof. The girls are unconscious for ten minutes. Rebecca is the first to come to, she's upside-down held in place by her seatbelt. The airbags have all gone off and there's a strong smell of gasoline. Rebecca looks over and she sees Hope's bloody face and that the dash has pinned her legs. She cries out, "Hope, wake up! Beverly where are you!?" Rebecca unbuckles her seatbelt and crashes down onto the roof of the truck head first. Both Rebecca's legs are broken and all of her right ribs. She feels the pain and screams out. She's looking up at Hope still in her seatbelt. Rebecca reaches out and nudges Hope but she does not respond. She starts doing it over and over yelling out, "Hope wake up, Hope wake up!! Please Hope wake up!" That's when Rebecca heard the sound, "WOOOF!" The truck was now on fire. Rebecca starts to panic, in pain she reaches up and unbuckles Hope's seatbelt, but the dashboard has her legs pinned, and she won't drop. Rebecca painfully screams at the top of her lungs saying, "Hope, Hope the trucks on fire wake up! Wake up!" Just then Rebecca feels hands grab her from behind and drag her out of the truck. As she's being dragged away by some good Samaritans, she is still screaming for her friend. The rescuers, two men, and a lady run back to the inflamed truck to try and remove Hope, in seconds they have to retreat due to the engulfed vehicle. Rebecca leaning holding her right side has to watch her friend burn in her uncles' truck. She cries out but her ribcage is excruciating, the physical and emotional pain is overwhelming, she flops back on the ground and passes out.

Rebecca feels a cool breeze, she opens her eyes and she's sitting in her spot overlooking the yellow ocean. Staring at the ocean, it begins to display memories of Hope and her. There are multiple series of experiences they've shared being shown as she remembers them. Tears start rolling down her cheeks as she sifts through the mental album of her life. Her face is one of defeat and sadness as the chronology unfolds. The Remaks appear just behind her and they softly say, "We are sorry Rebecca, We can see and feel how much Hope meant to you. What happened is not your fault." Moments pass and the Remaks turn to leave after not triggering a response. Then Rebecca still looking out at the ocean snidely says, "No it wasn't my fault, it was yours. You entered my life and I lost two people that were important to me within a week. At this rate, everyone I know and love will be gone in a month. You may be part of me, but I want no part of you. Stay out of my dreams, stay out of my life forever." The Remaks respond, "We…" They are instantly cut off as Rebecca screams, "FOREVER!!" The Remaks softly say, "As you wish…" Rebecca, goes back to reminiscing visions of her friend, within the tears there's brief spurts of weeping. This continues until Rebecca's consciously exhausted and goes into a deep sleep.

The television in the hospital room turns on and roams through channels stopping on the news, which is reporting on the accident on Caledonia Rd. Beverly watches from her bed, the mangled wreckage being recovered from the day prior. The reporter retells the incident.

"On Sunday, July 12th, a hate crime brought upon by a racist group based in Iowa. Stalked and terrorized the viral group called, "The Fearsome Threesome". Ultimately killing one by cutting their vehicle brakes line and running them off the road. The truck flipped seven times throwing one of the girls from the vehicle. Another was pulled from the wreckage by some passersby who were unable to save the third victim due to the vehicle becoming engulfed in flames. Two men were arrested in connection with the incident after they posted the video online. They are facing murder and attempted murder charges the district attorney said."

Beverly surfs channels for a lighter subject line, she decides on the movie Goonies that's just starting. Beverly has been awake off and on for about two hours. She's in a cervical neck/thoracic brace due to a broken spine. She looks over and sees Rebecca's fingers moving in the bed next to her. Beverly says, "You awake?" Rebecca has both her legs are in shin casts and her torso is bandaged tight. She asks groggy, "Beverly you're okay?" Rebecca sits up and looks over to her friend. Beverly sadly smiles and says, "Yea I'm okay but Hope didn't make it, love." Rebecca replies, "I know I saw her in the truck." Rebecca then swivels her legs to the ground and gets up angrily, "Those Fucking guys I'm gonna kill them!" Beverly interjects, "They already have them in custody. I guess it was some cult stalking us to kill us because of the...well you know." Rebecca plops back down on the bed and says, "What is wrong with people, Hope only ever wanted to help everyone. This is not fair." She sighs and says, "I'm losing it I can't take this much death. What the hell is going on in the world. The Remaks wanted me to save people because they were good. Fuck that, they are evil and should all perish there's no good in the world.' Rebecca turns back into the bed crying, 'I just want to go home." Beverly says, "You are good Rebecca you are the light remember." Rebecca fires back, "What the hell am I good at, I'm not the light, more like death's darkness. Saving everyone else and getting the people I love dead, yea that's what I'm good at obviously. You know what, where's the nurse I need to call my mom she probably worried sick." Beverly softly says, "You were still out an hour ago, I overheard the nurses say that your and my mom were on their way here." Rebecca breathes out and says, "I'm sorry Beverly, I haven't even asked how you are, I'm so sorry. How are you? Is your neck broken?" Beverly says, "I guess it was when the doctors brought me in, they said I was paralyzed from the neck down for life.' Beverly gets up out of bed unlatches the brace and drops it on the bed. 'Doctors... what do they know anyhow?" She then goes over and crawls into bed with Rebecca, each of the girls holding each other tight. Rebecca softly whimpers, "I'm sorry..." Beverly replies, "Me too..."

Maggie and Stella rush into the room to see their daughters cuddled up and they instantly start crying. The girls get up and begin with long hugs. Beverly starts helping Rebecca remove her bandages all while two doctors and nurses watch in amazement. One doctor stunned says to Beverly, "How?" Rebecca snarky, "believe me it's more of a curse than a blessing.' She looks at all of them, 'Can I get the saw, please to get these casts off me. I want to go home." The doctors and nurses leave to go get the saw, before the last one she leaves looks at Rebecca, and says, "Sorry truly, about your friend. We heard about you and what you were doing for people all the way up here. You are a blessing, keep it up, help as many as you can. Don't let the evil people get you down. My mother once told me don't let mean people mean anything to you. We are here for you." She shyly smiles and leaves the room. Rebecca smiles subtlety, at loss for words shakes her head as Maggie strokes her hair. The doctors return with the saw and proceeds to remove her cast. He's surprised at how quickly her shattered legs have completely healed. He says, "In all my years in medicine I've never seen anything like this."The other doctor inspects Beverly and is mesmerized to see her make a full recovery from a spinal injury. After moments of them being flabbergasted, Rebecca looks out the window. They are on the tenth floor she can see crowds of reporters waiting at the entrance. She does not want to deal with the scurry of fighting through reporters and cameras. She says, "The whole media empire is here, is there another way to get out of here Doc without dealing with them?" Maggie says, "Becca we didn't drive here. We took the helicopter." Rebecca says, "What? When did we get a helicopter?" Maggie replies, "Your dad." Rebecca surprised says, "Mr. Pendleton?" And at that time the suit-wearing Mr. Pendleton walks into the room and says, "At your service Ms. Marshall." Rebecca is internally relieved at the sight of him, for some reason as strong as she may be, Mr. Pendleton makes her feel safe. Everyone is directed to the rooftop helipad, where they are whisked into the midday sky for the flight home. It was another first-time experience for Rebecca that was afforded by her Dad via proxy, Mr. Pendleton. Again, taking her home and again after someone she loved died. This all made what should have been an exciting flight in a private helicopter, melancholy to say the least. Rebecca again just stared out of the window all the way home.

The helicopter lands in the backyard, everyone thanks Mr. Pendleton as they disembark. Before he leaves, he says to Rebecca, "Your dad really wishes he could have been here. I've known him a long time, he loves you and there's nothing he wouldn't do for you. He wants you to call him when you are ready." He then empathically says, "I'm sorry you lost your friend, your mom told me that she was an amazing human being." Rebecca sighs and says, "Okay and yea she was…one of a kind." Rebecca nods at him and turns to walk to the house. She hears the door slide shut and turbines grow louder, feeling the wind from the blades get stronger as she gets to the backdoor. The helicopter lifts off then disappears in the sky. Jordan is sitting in the kitchen as Rebecca comes in, he jumps up and gives his sister a big hug as tears roll down his cheek. Choking up he says, "I see you. Don't you ever scare me like that again. You're my sister, my hero, you're supposed to be invincible… I'm gonna miss Hope so much." They both start crying as they hold each other. Maggie, Beverly, Stella, and Professor Lambkin, who got there a day earlier. They're all looking at the siblings tightly embrace, sobbing over the tragedy. Rebecca says, "Has anyone talked to or gone to see Helen?" Helen was Hope's mother, there wasn't a father in the picture there also. Maggie says, "I spoke to her this morning and told her we were going to get you. I invited her but she was still in shock. Your father paid for Hope's remains to be flown to the mortuary by Uncle Ed's church, they'll be there later today." Rebecca woefully says, "I'm going to go see Helen." She then takes Maggie's car keys off the kitchen table and heads out the back door, softly saying, "Love you all…I'll be back soon."

At Hope's house, Rebecca finds Helen tilling away in her little tomato garden. Helen had mental issues for years. Her doctor recommended a subtle prescription plus gardening to help her cope with daily life. Rebecca had heard stories from Hope of her mother going off the deep end for minor infractions. Rebecca for sure thought this would be the ultimate crash for her… and it was. Walking up she saw Helen pruning some vines while humming, she softly says, "Hello Ms. Flowers." Helen looks up at Rebecca and jovially replies, "Oh hi Rebecca, Hope's not here right now, and can I do something for you?" Rebecca realizes that Helen is in denial, she asks, "So where is Hope, Ms. Flowers?" She replies, "Oh you know Hope, she's out there rescuing or doing a charity for something. That girl is such a giver. Don't worry, when she returns I'll be sure to pass the message along that you were here." Rebecca empathically smiles and says, "Okay thank you, Ms. Flowers." Rebecca turns to walk away and Helen says while still pruning, "You know she told me once that she was in love with you. Yea, she wanted you all to herself, that she'd marry you. That girl's so silly, yea she loved you, Becca. Oops!! I may have told a secret…Anyway, I'll be sure to tell her you were here. You have a good day now." A tear rolls down Helen's cheek as she smiles, Rebecca's eyes flood as she walks away. She whimpers back, "You too Ms. Flowers."

When Rebecca returns home at 4:10 pm, the house was quiet as can be. Beverly and Stella had gone home, Jordan was in his room. Maggie was in the kitchen with the professor, they weren't talking. He was just watching her make soup. Rebecca thought, are they an item now, she shook it off and just went to her room and closed the door, she crawled into bed fully clothed curled up and cried herself to sleep. News crews formed the next morning, Maggie called Rebecca's father who immediately hired a security company to come in and keep unwanted visitors off the property 24-7. Maggie didn't feel guilty for using Trevor for things she wanted, it was more like restitution to her. For the next few days, Rebecca basically stayed in her room, occasionally coming out to get food and go to the bathroom. When Friday came there was a soft knock on Rebecca's door around 7:30 am. The door opens and Maggie comes in and sits on the bed alongside Rebecca, "Today is Hope's funeral, I took care of all the arrangements for Helen, but I don't think she'll attend, you should come." Maggie kisses her daughter on the forehead and leaves softly shutting the door behind her. Rebecca takes a deep breath and grabs her phone. It had been turned off since she started hibernating days earlier. The phone boots up and she sees 232 missed messages. As she scrolls, it's all a bunch of "Get wells and sorry for your loss." It's interesting to see who some are from. Old friends, new friends, people who she didn't even know had her number. The whole high school football team. One special one from Quintin that reads;

"I just met you, I know we haven't really hung out and gotten to know each other really. But the second I found out something happened to you my heart dropped. So that must mean something. I'm very sorry about Hope, I'm giving you time to grieve but soon as you're ready I wanna come see you. Please text me back soon."

Rebecca smiles and texted him back, "You just brightened my day. I'll see you soon, I just need a little more time." A boyfriend was the last thing on her mind but for the moment any distraction was a good one. Rebecca got out of bed and went to the kitchen. Jordan was dabbling on the stove, he looks at her and in a feeble attempt to make her smile he says, "Gooooood morning Vietnam!" It was a line from a movie Rebecca liked. Rebecca hit back with, "Good morning, my neighbors." They both smile and then Jordan gets serious and softly asks, "Do you know what you are going to say today…at the funeral? I wrote some words down but it's hard for me to make sense of it. Rebecca tells her little brother, "Just speak from the heart, you can't go wrong if you do." She rubs his head then love taps him on the shoulder. They both sit down and enjoy the Mexican scrambled Huevos Jordan just made. Rebecca's impressed again she says, "Damn these are good!" Jordan replies, "I know right?!" The kids finish their food and commence to get ready for the sad inevitable.

At 11:30 am a black stretched Cadillac arrives to drive everyone to the church, paid for by you know who. The group walks to the car and the driver gets out and opens the door. As Rebecca enters the car, she's a little disappointed to not see Mr. Pendleton but instead, it's a handsome very well-dressed man, he offers Rebecca to sit next to him. As Maggie enters the car you see the look of surprise on her face, catching herself she says with poise, "Thank you for all you've done for us Trevor, it was nice of you." Rebecca looks at the man, "You're my father?" He replies, "My name is Trevor Washington, and it's a pleasure to finally meet you, Rebecca." He puts out his hand to shake hers and she lunges to hug him. Maggie and Jordan watch on as the separated two reunite. After Rebecca releases her hold she asks where's Mr. Pendleton he's been so good to me. At this time the divider rolls down and Mr. Pendleton from the front passenger seat says, I'm here Ms. Marshall at your service. Rebecca smiles and the car drives off to the church.

The drive to the church was a little awkward, Maggie wouldn't look at Trevor whereas Rebecca and Jordan couldn't stop looking at him. Rebecca laughs out loud and cynically says, "FML, as a kid I dreamed of the day my mom and dad would be together and we'd go for drives. It finally happens and it's to my best friend's funeral… Life's a trip, Que no?" Trevor inserts, "Um, I hope you all don't mind me going to her funeral. I understand if it's a problem." Maggie shrugs and Rebecca says, "I appreciate you being here, thank you."

The Cadillac arrives at the church and everyone enters, Mrs. Sarah is on the organ playing melodic background hymns. They make their way down the aisle, the front pew is reserved for the Marshall family and Helen. Rebecca sits between her mom and dad with Jordan next to Maggie. The church doesn't hold but 100 people and it was maybe half full. This was intentional, the funeral was not broadcasted to the public. After Uncle Pete's they wanted a small ceremony so is to not make a spectacle of Hope's passing. The people in attendance were some school friends and past people Hope had helped and touched with her kindness. As the ceremony proceeded everyone talked said their peace, then it was Rebecca's turn. On the podium, she looks over the crowd and says, "I didn't write anything down because I wanted this to come, on the spot from my heart. Now I can't think what to say or how to begin.' She pauses for a moment and clears her throat, 'Hope was my best friend since I was ten. But she was more than that, she was my inspiration, my confidant, my wingman, she was my Goose. She was tragically taken away from me, us ... and now the world is a sadder place because of her death. I admit I'm a little lost without her, I think I'll always be. But you don't have to be, do as she did and help someone with a problem, lend a hand, and give money to a good cause. Do this and Hope is in your heart where she belongs.' She turns and looks at the casket, 'I love you and miss you, and yes, I would have married you." Rebecca bends over kisses the casket then walks off the podium and back to her seat. Maggie is a little shocked by her last statement but just smiles all the same.

With the ceremony done and everyone walks to their respected cars from the burial site. Jordan walks briskly up to Rebecca, puzzled asks, "Are you gay?" Rebecca laughs, "So how long have you been holding that one in?" Jordan stammers, "Well since you just told the whole congregation you'd marry a girl. That's how long...!" Rebecca trying to ease her brother, "Relax I'd still be your big sister." She grabs him and they hug as they walk to the car. Once inside she makes sure the seating is where Maggie is right next to Trevor trying to force a conversation between them. The Caddy begins to pull out of the parking spot and Rebecca says aloud, "Okay you two need to resolve whatever's between you because I need you both in my life now.' She calls out, 'Mr. Pendleton..." He responds, "Yes Ms. Marshall." She commands, "I need you to make sure they do not get out of this car till they are civil with each other. Can you do that?" Mr. Pendleton replies, "Will do Ms. Marshall." Trevor looks at Mr. Pendleton and he shrugs his shoulders, "You told me to do as she asks." Rebecca looks out the back car window and screams out, "STOP! I need to get out." She opens the car door before the car comes to a complete stop, jumps out saying, "Don't wait for me I'll find a way home." Then she shuts the door and hurries back to the church. The grave site was empty except for one person, someone she did not see the whole ceremony, Helen. As Rebecca got closer Helen sat on the grass next to her buried daughter, her yellow dress spread out like a flower around her. Rebecca slowly walks up, then sits beside Helen not saying a word to her. Helen looks at her and says, "I heard what you said, Hope would have wanted nothing more. Thank you for loving my daughter. Will you sit with me awhile?" Rebecca smiles, "I'll stay here as long as you like." She reaches out and holds Helen's hand.

It's a moment they both needed as a few tears slowly run down their cheeks.

It was 4:22 pm when Uncle Ed dropped Rebecca home. He also dropped Helen home, they tried to convince her to come over and have dinner. But she'd taken on as much as she could in one day and just wanted her garden now. Rebecca saw that the black Cadillac was still here and thought, "Well that's a good sign...right?" She and Uncle Ed walk into the house, the driver, Mr. Pendleton, and Trevor are all in the living room along with Maggie and Professor Lambkin. Rebecca just keeps trotting by straight to the kitchen, where she finds her brother cooking. She says, "When I thought this day couldn't get any weirder, the Professor shows up." Jordan says, "Yea and they've all been laughing it up in there like old friends, it's weird." Just then Maggie yells, "Becca can you come in here for a minute please?" Rebecca looks at her brother, "Oh oh they're gonna drag me into their commune. Wish me luck." Rebecca walks in all smiley-faced and says, "Good to see you all getting along." Maggie says, "Your father and I have made up, he wants to ask you a question." Rebecca turns to him and says, "Yes?" Trevor stands up and says, "How would you like to get away for a week and stay with me at my home in New York City?" Rebecca blindsided drops down on the couch. She sits there pondering, Jordan burst through the kitchen door, "I'll go I'll go, the best chefs are there." Everyone laughs. Rebecca, excited, graciously says, "Yes, I'll go. Thank you." Rebecca is still mourning her friend and uncle, it's hard for her to be happy when deep down she's in so much pain. Everything starts becoming a distraction to how she's really feeling. She says, "New York wow! The Big Apple, Times Square, the Empire State, Broadway...' jokingly confident she says, 'I hope they're ready for me? Trevor laughs "Rebecca, they have no clue, you're gonna bring down the house." She smiles.

The night proceeds with cordial conversations. Rebecca finds out that her father is filthy rich. He's a real estate developer worth billions, his trusted sidekick Mr. Pendleton is not just a lawyer but ex-Special Forces and not someone to mess with. In hearing this Rebecca can't help herself she says, "I suppose we have to register you as a lethal weapon." Her dad hurriedly says, "Lethal Weapon!" Everyone laughs and Jordan says, "She does that a lot," Maggie chimes in, "A lot, she's a little movie junkie." They all smile as Rebecca shrugs her shoulders and smiles. It's a night that the whole family needed, some healing, uniting, and laughter.

After dinner, Trevor leaves with his companions but not before telling Rebecca he's sorry for not being there and promises to spend the rest of his life making up for the lost time. He tells her that he has to go back to New York tonight but that he'll send Mr. Pendleton in the helicopter to pick her up tomorrow at noon. She agrees, gives her dad an extra-long hug then they leave. Back in the house, Rebecca goes up to her mom as she's doing the dishes and hugs her. "Thanks, mom for letting me go to New York." Maggie scoffs it off and says, "I was getting tired of you hanging around here anyhow, go bother your father for a while see how he likes it." Rebecca smiles gives her another squeeze, and says, "Love you too." Then she goes to her room. She falls asleep shortly after. In her dream spot, she's overlooking the ocean like normal. She's not as angry with the Remaks as before and subtlety peeks behind into the darkness to see if are there. She's a little disappointed to see just a dark void and turns back to look at her horizon. As she sits behind her there's a faint purple light that appears and slowly fades away.

chapter twelve

OLIVER

Rebecca didn't need her alarm to wake her on this particular morning. She was up and packed by 8 am. She filled a backpack with some shorts, tops, and essentials and was ready to go. She texted Quintin and Beverly, "Gonna spend some time with my dad in New York C U when I get back." Maggie had bittersweet feelings about Rebecca leaving and it became worse as noon rolled around. They could hear the helicopter getting closer and closer. It landed in the backyard and Mr. Pendleton exited with the blades still turning. He walks up to Rebecca whose backpack is ready standing with her mom and Jordan. He says, "Your chariot awaits." She turns back and sees her mom's eyes watering up and hugs her as she says, "Mom don't cry, I'll be back before you know it." Maggie trying to hold it in says, "I know Becca, just be careful okay. I love you." Rebecca replies, "I love you too mom." She looks at Jordan, "Next time you can come with me." And winks at him. Jordan happily, "Hell yea!" Rebecca then hugs Jordan laughs and says, "I have to... get to the Choppa!" she high fives him and hurries her way into the helicopter.

As the helicopter lifts off, Mr. Pendleton hands her a head set to communicate through. She asks, "How long till we get there?" He replies, "We are flying to Windsor International Airport then taking a jet to JFK, about 2hrs total travel time." Rebecca excitedly screams out, "Holy Crap!" She is stricken with a perma smile. She goes on to ask Mr. Pendleton question after question about things he's done in his life. She finds out that she horrifically met her dad. Fifteen years ago Mr. Pendleton was getting a drink from a convenience store. Some kids came in with a gun trying to rob the place. Mr. Pendleton stepped in to prevent it and was shot. Rebecca's dad was in the store at the time and rushed him to the hospital which saved his life. In the days it took to heal, Trevor would stop in from time to time to see how he was doing. They became friends, and so happens Mr. Pendleton didn't have a job at the time. He had just gotten out of the military and looking for something to do. Trevor was busy making his fortune and needed someone he trusted to be his head of security, so Trevor hired him. Their friendship grew and now Mr. Pendleton handles specific duties for her father, with his very particular set of skills. She learned he had recently passed the Bar exam, had no kids, and was dating a swimsuit model. And from the way he talked, he really would do anything for her father. The exchange of stories continued throughout the whole flight until they landed at John F. Kennedy Airport. Rebecca could not stop looking out of the plane window at the Big Apple skyline. This only was intensified when they got picked up by another helicopter to take them from the airport to Manhattan. Mr. Pendleton had the pilot buzz the city a little so Rebecca could get a birds-eye view. When they landed at Downtown Heliport, Trevor was waiting with a car for them. Trevor and Rebecca sat in the back seat while the driver and Mr. Pendleton sat up front. It was 2:32 pm and a beautiful warm summer day in the city. As they drive through the city she can see places she only saw in movies. She says to her dad, "It's so much more than what you see in movies." Trevor replies, "Yeah it is. Are you hungry for some pizza, I know a great place?" Ecstatically she says, "Oh my god New York pizza. I wanna fold it and have the grease run down my arm." Trevor laughs. "Can we go to Central Park?" she asks. He replies, "Sure... how about you make a list of places you want to go this week and we'll cross as many as we can off the list." Grinning ear to ear she says, "Deal!"

They drive to the pizza parlor where Rebecca has 2 slices with grease running. Then they hit Central Park and walk around seeing the live acts and hundreds of tourists. Mr. Pendleton walks a few feet behind them as they make their way. Trevor's face is well known in the city but as they walk its Rebecca that people a keying into. A lot are pointing and a few even approaches her saying, "Are you her?" That's when Mr. Pendleton steps in and guides them away. But the kicker is everyone is recording them walking through the park. Instead of walking around the park, Trevor has the driver meet them at another exit out of the park. Its 6:15 pm, Trevor tells Rebecca that he has a surprise for her back at his house. She laughs, "What? A pony…" Jokingly he says, "No Beyoncé." She stammers, "You're Shitting me?" He replies, "Yeah I'm shitting you. But I could arrange a meet and greet if you like, whenever she's not busy." Rebecca is beside herself, "Holy crap my dad is the King of New York." They laugh as they all get back in the car.

It takes twenty minutes to get to Trevor's place in Manhattan. Mr. Pendleton lives in the same building, just a lower floor. Rebecca is in awe as she walks through the lobby of where her father lives. There's a fountain with large Koi fishes in the center, giant modern art paintings hanging on the walls, and a large botanical garden in the corner. It's all so modern she thought to herself. They get to the elevator and as they are waiting a mother and son join them. The elevator dings and they enter. The kid while holding his mother's hand, is looking at Rebecca and she smiles. He's wearing a Beanie, Rebecca has seen this before in a couple of kids she helped. She says, "Hi, nice beanie." He looks at his mom and she says, "It's not polite not to say hi back." The little boy looks at Rebecca and says, "Hi." Rebecca says, "I'm Rebecca, what's your name?" Shyly he says, "My name is Oliver, I'm six…and I'm sick that's why I wear the Beanie if you were wondering." Rebecca responds, "Well it's a pretty cool beanie." At that time the elevator stopped on the 7th floor, dings and the door opens. As they walk out Oliver says, "Bye Rebecca." Waving she says, "Bye Oliver, nice to meet you." The doors shut and Mr. Pendleton says, "I see them sometimes, poor kid has had cancer since he was three." The elevator dings again and Mr. Pendleton says, "It's a pleasure getting to know you Rebecca, welcome to New York." He nods at Trevor and exits the elevator. Rebecca turns to her dad, "So where's your floor?" He then takes out a card and swipes the penthouse pad. Rebecca rolls her eyes, "Yea I should have known that." The elevator dings for the last time and the doors open to a house she only sees in the movies. It's an 8000sq foot penthouse taking up the top two floors of a 100 story building, along with the roof which has a pool. Trevor shows her around the modern décor styled home. The living room is bigger than her entire house back home. She then asks, "So where's my surprise?" He then leads her upstairs to an empty corner room with a view of the Statue of Liberty. In the middle of the vacant room lies an arrangement of catalogs, Trevor looks at Rebecca, "This is your room, you can go through those catalogs and furnish it however you please. I would have done it myself but I figured you'd probably enjoy this more." Rebecca excitedly lunges and gives her dad a big hug, "Oh my god are you serious? Thank you this is amazing." She runs around the 500sq ft. room yelling out, "Holy crap the bathroom is bigger than my bedroom back home." She then walks up to Trevor and gratefully says, "Thanks, dad." He then embraces Rebecca after hearing her call him dad for the first time, "No thank you. I love you kiddo, you are the special piece that was missing in my life." He kisses her forehead, "Tomorrow morning at 8, an interior decorator is coming to see you, to help you with your room. For tonight you can stay in the guest bedroom down the hall. In the closet, there's something your mom helped me pick out for you to wear to dinner tonight. I hope you like it." Rebecca a little overwhelmed takes a selfie of the view from her new bedroom and posts it with the tag, "Wolf of Wall Street Bitches!!"

In the closet of the guest room, Rebecca finds an elegant yet simple white dress, something she could see her mom picking out for her. She takes out her phone and calls her mom, after two rings Maggie answers. Rebecca thanks her for the selection, it eases Maggie's mind knowing she's safe. Rebecca knew her mom wouldn't be able to rest until she heard from her. They exchange I love you and hang up. Rebecca stands in front of the full-length window overlooking the historic city and she smiles and sighs at its grandeur. She then throws her phone on the bed and goes into the bathroom to get ready. After a shower she dons her new dress, she looks at herself in the mirror and twirls around she's beginning to see herself as a young woman, discarding the robe of a tomboy, she feels pretty. Rebecca walks into the giant living room to find her dad waiting. He changed his clothes also and now is dressed in a fitted grey suit. He greets his daughter and says, "Daughter, would you like to join me for dinner on the rooftop?" She replies, "I would like nothing more father." They both laugh. Trevor shows her to the elevator and Rebecca exclaims, "You seriously have an elevator in your house…" He looks at her and comes back with, "Technically this house is yours also so…" She stammers and laughs, "I have an elevator in my house… very cosmopolitan." The elevator dings and the doors open. As they walk out its Rebecca's first time on the rooftop. She feels the cool summer breeze and even though they are high up, she can still hear the horns from the busy city below. The roof lighting is soft as to not take away from the skyline view. There's a straight bar alongside the right of the pool, which is a mini Olympic size with a built-in Jacuzzi on the left side. Trevor says, "Do you swim?" Rebecca being a smart ass replies, "Um I just got my arm a couple of weeks ago…so no." Her dad smiles, "My apologies, well that's something we'll have to remedy, isn't it?" She looks at him a little bit bewildered, "Did you just quote Braveheart?" Trevor says, "It's kinda my thing too." She gasps, "This is all so crazy, a month ago I was just a kid about to graduate high school and then figure out what I was gonna do with my life. Fast-forward, and now have super powers lost my best friend and uncle…and apparently reside in a high rise apartment in the greatest city in the world… I'm Batman!" They both laugh and Trevor says, "And I'll be your Alfred… Miss right this way." He shows her to a table where a waiter waits. Dinner goes on and the two swap stories about movies, food, and life. The overdue meeting goes well into the night as father and daughter bond. Rebecca was happy for the moment.

Rebecca woke up at 7 am, her eyes opened to being a little puzzled at first until she remembered where she was. She goes into the kitchen where she sees her dad already making scrambled eggs with pep he says, "Good morning sunshine. You like scrambled eggs, right?" Rebecca nods, "Yes that's fine, thank you." "The decorator will be here shortly his name is Stephan and how should I say… he's a little exuberant but very good at what he does." She nods again smiling, "Can't wait to meet him." Breakfast continues like dinner as the two get carried away connecting Trevor's phone chimes, it's Stephan. He's in the elevator and needed access to the penthouse. Trevor taps the release button on his phone. Rebecca says, "I was wondering how you got visitors up here." "Yep and there's a camera so I can see whose coming up also," Trevor adds. The elevator doors open and a 35yr old Caucasian man with eyeliner dressed in a Gucci blouse and shorts with gem rings on every finger. Hurries his way through the house calling out for Trevor. Trevor answers, "We're in the kitchen." Stephan enters and immediately greets Rebecca, "Hello doll, well don't you resemble your beautiful father. What's your name sweetheart?" Stephan reminds her of a gay Robin Williams. "Rebecca." She replies chuckling. "It is a pleasure meeting you I am Stephan Poindexter III. I hear you have a room that you need, to fit your style. How about we excuse ourselves and spend some of your daddy's money girlfriend." Stephan grabs Rebecca's hand and drags her out of the kitchen. Her dad laughing, just looks at her and shrugs his shoulders. He throws in, "Hey I have to go into work but I'm sending a car to pick you up at noon so we can have lunch together." She replies from down the hall, "Okay Daddy, love you." Trevor walking out of the kitchen with a grin says to himself, "I'll never get tired of that."

Time seemed to fly by and noon came quick. The two worked out some ideas on what she wanted and Stephan left typing away on his phone making orders for furniture, lighting, rugs and a California king bed. She didn't need that big of a bed, but it was for Hope. She like having room and pretending her best friend was always sleeping with her. Rebecca was barely ready and running out of the guest room when the elevator opened and Mr. Pendleton was there. He says, "Good afternoon Rebecca, I'm here to escort you to your father." "Hi Mr. Pendleton, awesome! Are you joining us for lunch too?" "If you like?" He replies. "I insist." She says as doors close. On the way down the elevator stops on the 7th floor and Oliver and his mom get on. Oliver happily says, "Hi Rebecca." Smiling she replies, "Hi Oliver where are you off to?" "I have to go get my treatment, I hate these days." Rebecca's smile fades away to a look of concern then she covers it up by energetically saying, "Do you know how to swim?" His eyes light up and he says, "I sure can!!" She replies, "I can't but I have a pool do you wanna come show me how?" Amazed he asks, "Do you live on the top floor?" Rebecca replies, "I sure do. So what say you, when are you done with your treatment?" His mom says, "He should be home at 2:30 pm we'll see how he feels sometimes it takes a lot out of him. But we'll see." The elevator opens to the first floor and Oliver waves' bye to Rebecca, "See ya later alligator." "After while crocodile." Rebecca hollers back.

In the car drive to her dad's work, Rebecca couldn't stop thinking about Oliver. She wanted to heal him but she hadn't tried to fix anyone since the orb left. She didn't even know how to and did she really want to open up that world again. No one had really engaged her for fixing since the orb left, it was kinda a relief she liked feeling normal again. She still wondered though could she do it if she tried. This weighed on her all through lunch, even though she was amongst her dad and Mr. Pendleton her mind was in the little boy with cancer. They finished lunch and Trevor took his daughter to the Guggenheim Museum and up to the One World observatory. Rebecca was in love with New York, it had so much to offer everyone, and in her mind she wanted Oliver to live to see it all.

It was 4:45pm when they returned home from sightseeing. As they walked through the lobby Oliver's mom who was impatiently waiting, runs to Rebecca and in a panic says, "It's you, you're that girl, and I just saw a clip on the internet about you. Please help my Oliver he's upstairs in so much pain, please help my son! I'll give you anything, don't let him die." People in the lobby have now taken notice. In New York, everyone typically doesn't pay attention to anyone unless something happens to draw said attention, and even then most people go about their own business. This was not one of those things. People started getting closer and videoing with their phones. Rebecca looks at Oliver's mother seeing the pure desperation in her eyes and says, "Take me to him." They all four dashes to the elevator, the crowd records their every move. While in the elevator Rebecca says openly, "I haven't fixed anyone since the orb left, I don't know if I can heal anyone without it." The mom pleads, "Just please try." Rebecca nods.

They all quietly enter Oliver's room and see him sleeping in a hospital bed surrounded by various types of monitors. His mother gently nudges him awake, "Oli wake up there's someone here to see you." Oliver slowly opens his little eyes, "Hi Rebecca, I'm sorry but I don't think I can show you how to swim right now, maybe tomorrow."

Rebecca says, "Oh that's okay I just wanted to see you and say hi." Oliver groggy says, "Mom can I have some water please." "Yes dear," She replies. His mom pours from a pitcher on the dresser and helps him sip from the glass. She says, "Okay Oli, Rebecca is going to try and help you, okay." He nods, "Okay." She moves out of the way and Rebecca stands next to him. She rests her hand on his and tries forcing her gift on him…nothing happens. She then tries touching his head with the same result, Rebecca hastily starts touching and squeezing with no effect. Oliver quietly says, "It's alright Rebecca I still believe that you are the light, maybe it's just my time." Then unexpectedly Oliver starts convulsing, his mother comes forward, "It's the tumor in his brain he has like 3 seizures a day, we need to just wait it out." All four adults watch as the kid suffers through his agony. Rebecca fed up with watching, says, "No more…" She closes her eyes and slows her breathing down concentrating on the things the Remaks told her. Then it happened, the darkness in a flash had light. With her eyes closed, she could see Oliver's orange aura as he lay on the bed. She could also see the cancer living in his brain with its grey aura. Rebecca touches Oliver's forehead and sees her white light engulf the grey and bond with the orange aura. She opens her eyes and sees Oliver looking up at her laughing he excitedly says, "That was cool can I do it again?" She laughs, "No I'm afraid it's only a one time deal.' Rebecca steps back in relief, 'Phew, I did it." Rebecca turns around happy as can be only to see three adults with their mouths dropped. The mother comes out of it first and runs to her son, Mr. Pendleton is just shaking his head with his eyes wide. Trevor then says, "What was that? How did you do that? The flash was so bright?" Rebecca little confused, "What did you see?" "You reached out and touched Oliver's head and there was a giant flash of white light, I'm still seeing spots," Trevor says rubbing his eyes. "Dad, it was way more than that, I'll explain later.' She turns to the kid, 'The good news is Oliver you're fixed, the cancer is no more." His mother crying hugs Rebecca, "Thank you, I am forever in your debt." "No thank you, you don't owe me anything, I have this ability for a reason… this is the reason. If anything, I owe you for making me realize my purpose again. Hope was the one that kept me focused, I guess without her I lost sight. But no more, I'm back.' She looks at her dad, 'Dad, can I use the money you were gonna spend to furnish my room, to instead build me a facility in Flint so I can treat those that need help?" Trevor looks at his daughter and her selflessness and says, "I think we may be able to do both.' He looks at the mother, 'Let's leave Ms....?" She replies, "Oh my god, I'm Judith sorry I didn't realize I never introduced myself." "Hi Judith, I'm Trevor and this gentleman is Mr. Pendleton." Mr. Pendleton reaches his hand out to greet her and says, "Just call me John." Rebecca did not know his first name, so she had a surprised look on her face. Trevor did, he just looks at him and laughs it off.

Back up in the penthouse Rebecca and her dad went over ideas while eating pizza then ice cream. He decides to construct a whole non-profit facility for her. And he used his high-up connections to ensure that his daughter would be safe and free to go about her endeavor as she pleased. They explored the city each day she was there and found out they had so much inherently in common, it was no mistake that Rebecca was his daughter.

For a while Rebecca had been dreaming of other random things, that night she visited her old spot overlooking the golden ocean. As she sat, smiled and called out, "You can come out you know I won't bite." The glowing figure emerges out of the darkness, "Hello Rebecca." She replies, "I've missed you, I was being a brat, I'm sorry for lashing out at you, it was very mean of me. I hope you can forgive me." The Remaks softly respond, "We understand...there's nothing to forgive." She asks, "Will you sit with me?" The Remaks sit next to her and say, "We feel the pain you are feeling. We also feel the joy in your heart when you do what you do. Your light shines so brightly when you're happy." Rebecca chuckles, "You still believe I'm here to save everyone, how is that even possible." "You'll find a way...and as you can see you're not alone." They reply. A few moments go by and she lovingly says, "I'm glad you're here." The Remaks softly, "We never left." Rebecca then says quietly, "For Hope..."

chapter thirteen

HOPE'S PLACE

After a joyous week with her father, Rebecca returned to Flint with a rejuvenated mindset. Trevor sent out surveyors and an architect to design a building on a plot of land he purchased from the city. Construction was going to take three months putting completion around the end of October beginning November. In the meantime, Trevor rented an old motel that held 6 rooms a few miles from the Marshall residence for Rebecca to conduct fixings. The motel was gated and had an empty lot next to it where people could use to park. He hired 24hr armed security and made sure the governor would not allow any government agencies to interfere with her, his deep pockets afforded him a lot of powerful influence. Judith also made a substantial donation to help get them up and running. Oliver was now cancer-free and she was more than happy to contribute to the cause. Beverly was hired as the coordinator, she managed a staff that took appointments, did advertising, and arranged catering of services from a local business. Hotels in the area had shuttles bussing people to and fro, food trucks would line the road for incoming guests. They also had an assortment of bakeries that would take turns supplying the motel weekly with treats for the guests. The word was spreading like wildfire about the Fixer, people were driving and flying in to see Rebecca from every corner of the planet. The 1 percenters of the earth would even offer to fly Rebecca to come fix them, but she had the policy of everyone being treated the same. They would all have to come and wait for their turn no matter creed nor color rich or poor. The doors would open Monday-Friday, 8 am-11 am then 1 pm-10 pm and on Saturday 8 am-3 pm. It was also still a donation based so all could afford it. Rebecca used the motel rooms to fix each guest, if they had no place to stay they could sleep it off the process at the motel. Each guest took about 20min to be seen. Everyone was told to watch a YouTube video that explained the origin story along with testimonials from past Fixees, to prepare them for what was about to take place. A consent form would have to be signed by each Fixee, this protected Rebecca and what she was doing from reprisal. It seems greed was still a biological basis that even the Remaks gift could not remove. A few Fixees tried going on media outlets saying they were tricked into the touch and now were having adverse effects. Trevor had five lawyers who so happened were touched and therefore were enlightened. They send out cease and desist letters with heavy ramifications to the individuals. This quickly squash their complaints, but the damage was done, once the conspiracy peddlers got ahold of the story, they created hysteria. And as with anything the protesters followed, they would picket across the street every day chanting words of discouragement. No one was ever persuaded by their torment, sometimes there'd be a confrontation, but the cops would hurry and remove the aggressors. Rebecca would sometimes offer them some of the baked goods, they always declined her "Alien Cookies", she'd just smile and leave the plate just in case they changed their mind. Her father always had a security detail pick her up and drive her wherever she went. At first, it was annoying but she understood because of what happened to Hope. She just never pictured herself having her own Kingsman secret service, it made her feel like the president.

November came fast, along with the cold weather, but the facility was finally complete. Rebecca from its conception knew what it would be called when finished, Hope's Place. There just wasn't a more fitting name for a place that gave hope to those without. And Rebecca wanted to pay tribute to her friend that she missed every day that went by. The building was one story, 10000sq. ft. with twenty mini bedrooms. They were set up like a hotel room, sink, bathroom/shower, etc. for all that may stay. There was a waiting room with massage chairs and some twin beds, for whoever waiting could sit. Televisions hung all over showing multiple programs. There were pictures on the walls that past Fixees sent showing them enjoying their new least on life. The walls were painted in soft happy tones as to comfort the guest, it was a place Rebecca wished Hope would approve of. The building was heavily fenced in and four armed security guards manned the gated entrance. They checked each guest for weapons and contraband and they were serious, her own private TSA. The outside lot was set up for 100 parking spots and an area where the food trucks could post, along with an indoor eating area for the guest. Beverly hired fifteen people to help inside that includes three nurses, one of them being Maggie "Head Nurse". The rest were helpers and reception who collected the donations. There were other hires of a custodial nature and Trevor took care of all the security staff. It was a crisp sunny afternoon on November 20th that the ribbon-cutting occurred, the governor and a few senators were in the audience. Trevor and Mr. Pendleton were also in attendance along with the Marshall clan. Rebecca received the key to the city from the mayor, who still hadn't been touched. She cut the red ribbon as two white doves were released one for Hope and the other for her Uncle Pete. Rebecca finally felt ready to take on this impossible task of saving the world.

The first month of Hope's Place was hectic, the influx of people was beyond expectation. Chaos in the parking lot resulted in someone being shot by another guest, luckily they survived. Even Uncle Ed tried helping. He would roam the parking lot trying to keep the peace through prayer. The police had to hire special detail to handle the drones of people flocking to Flint. This all put a new light on Flint Michigan. The federal government funded a bill to immediately start the removal and clean-up of all the toxic waste and material. Environmental groups were there restructuring the development of vegetation and wildlife. Money was being pumped into Flint like a hot Las Vegas slot machine.

The second month was just as bad at Hope's Place. Rebecca was getting burnt out also. Social media played its part on both sides of the love-hate coin. Some hateful memes would pop up and she would see making her feel discouraged. But the moment she'd fix a child or a last hope person it would all disappear. She knew haters are gonna hate no matter what. One good thing that came out of social media was a follower called Mike Jones. He floated the idea of a lottery, where sick people register and are given a number. The number is then entered into a daily lottery where there are 36 winners every day. The winners are then given a future appointment date, this would regulate the flow and limit the chaos yet still make it fair to all. This idea went viral fast and of course, Trevor helped contract a tech agency to carry out the worldwide registry. It took 3 weeks to create, test, and retest the software for glitches. A central computer handled the lottery and satellite stations around the world were set up to store the encrypted data. The first month of its implementation felt like a calm after a storm. There were still the street drama and an occasional straggler trying to cut in line but for the most part, thing flowed smooth. Rebecca personally rewarded Mike Jones with a BMW of his choosing for his brilliant idea, he was much appreciative.

The time now seemed to roll on faster months turn into years and years turned into decades. Around decade number two Rebecca had almost touched 180000 people. Though 20yrs had passed, she only aged 10. Throughout the time she took a week here and there to give herself a break. Vacationing in Thailand and an African Safari was two memorable vacations for her. Every time she'd come home, there'd be a sea of people to greet her at the airport and line the roadways to wave at her as her car drove by. Not even the president of the United States or Pope was this loved. Within the 20yrs span, the effects of the Remakes splice surfaced. People were only able to get pregnant every five years. This might have been a problem but people were living longer, having babies too often would create overpopulation. Once this was indoctrinated into society it started to become more and more appreciated…but not by all. A few domestic terrorist groups would occasionally try to bomb the building or take shots at the Marshall house. Which resulted in a 6ft cinderblock wall to be built around the house. Only Maggie and Professor Lambkin lived there now. Rebecca got married to Quintin and lived in a guarded private mansion provided by none other than Trevor. Jordan became a chef and ran two restaurants, one high-class fine dining and the other a fusion of comfort food. So happened the restaurants were direct across the street from each other in downtown Flint. Jordan would also when asked, help out the fire department and police in search and rescue missions due to his extraordinary eyesight. It was November 16th, 2040, the world was focused on Rebecca, wars and conflicts took a backseat to health and living. The people who had been touched went on to excel in everything they did. Engineers and technology jumped leaps and bounds in the past ten years. With governments funding billions of dollars towards each country's space program. Astronomers were able to see and explore so much more of the universe than ever before. Guess everyone was racing to find the next celestial visitor. The world seemed to be looking through a fresh pair of glasses, there was hope for the future. Rebecca was realizing what the Remaks knew all along, she was the one that made this all happen. She was humankind's savior... and on November 17th, 2040 at 2:07pm this savior would wish she'd never been born.

chapter fourteen

ROSEMARY'S DEN

"Quintin where's my blue chucks?" Rebecca yells from the bedroom closet. "They are where you left them…front door closet," Quintin yells back from the kitchen. He was making a quick breakfast of a bagel and cream cheese for them both. It was 7:30am November 17th, 2040 and they were running late. They had a long night attending a gala for a charity event to help construct a new park on land that was once contaminated, but since reclaimed. Rebecca runs to the front door closet grabs her sneakers, puts them on and hurries into the kitchen. "Babe I gotta go." She says as she kisses him. "Okay finish this on the drive," Quintin says as he hands her the bagel and coffee. She replies, "I will, love you, figure out where you want to go for dinner tonight." as she runs out the door. It's Saturday and Rebecca always liked celebrating the end of the work week with dinner at a nice restaurant. Her favorite food was still Italian, so Quintin on reflex because they are frequently there, yells out, "Lorenzo's?" as the front door shuts. The House responds, "Sir what time would you like me to make the reservations for, and how many people." "Sally make it for two at 5:30 pm.' Quintin replies, 'Sally what time is my tee time today?" "Your tee time at Sandstone Golf Course is at 8:15 am. You have five minutes to leave to make it on time." The House says. "Oh shit, I gotta go!" Quintin gasps out as he runs for the door. "Sally lock up the house." "I will sir, have a good golf day." The House replies.

Rebecca's drive into work this Saturday was typical. She greeted her driver and security detail as she entered the car. They were a no shit-taking outfit who took their job seriously in protecting her. In her car there were two, Rebecca always drove in the backseat. They were followed by a chase car with three additional sentries. In the last 20yrs she had only two details protecting her and within that time eight altercations. And of the eight, only one time there was gun fire. August 2029, a lone gunman tried ambushing them at a stoplight. The gunman ran up to Rebecca's car with an Uzi and delivered a barrage of bullets. It was futile, the car was fully armored, and the chase car detail jumped out of their vehicle and put the man down with six shots. Rebecca witnessed it all and was quite traumatized. She saw the man's eyes as he took his last breath and she felt sorry for him. She did not know him and never found out why he tried to kill her, it was a bad day for all…and today would be worse.

As the car rolled through the winter countryside, she was harboring a little secret that she was going to reveal to Quintin over dinner later. Rebecca had a smile on her face as she ate her bagel and sipped her coffee. This was the first time she'd gotten pregnant; she was four months along with a Humak baby i.e. human and Remak cross breed. Pregnancy with Humak babies lasted 12 months to come to term, she was due in July. This was the fourth opportunity to get pregnant since Rebecca first touched the orb and right now, she felt ready to bring her child into the world. She was so happy, only Beverly knew currently, she had to tell somebody and Beverly was her oldest and best good friend. Beverly was still the head honcho at Hope's Place. She had grown up a lot, she now wore expensive women's business suits and attended board meetings all day, a far cry from her former. Rebecca felt on top of the world as the car entered the facility, it was a beautiful clear cool November morning.

Walking into the building she greeted, "Good Morning" to everyone she passed by. Her assistant was already in her office, ready to brief her on her first appointment with Mr. Benjamin. Rebecca says, "Good morning Claire." "Good morning Mrs. Marshall. I have your first appointment Mr. Benjamin from Toronto Canada he's suffering from severe Rheumatoid Arthritis." Claire replies. Rebecca puts on the medical white coat hanging in the coat rack. Studies showed people are more at ease if they see someone there to help them are in a doctor's jacket... so she wore one. She says, "How was your date last night?" Claire replies, "He was nice, but no sparks. I have another guy tonight...we'll see how it goes." Rebecca laughs, "What? Look at you playing the field, that's right never settle, life's long, enjoy the ride.' She high fives her, "What room is Mr. Benjamin in?" Claire responds, "Room 5." Rebecca walks out as Claire follows to room 5. They greet the waiting gentlemen and proceed with the fixing process.

The day plays out like any normal day. The staff always promoted a happy, positive environment to the guests. Helping people was great, but it was Saturday, which meant a day off Sunday, and who doesn't like a day off. The waiting area always smelled of fresh-baked cookies and cakes, if anything, people could complain the place was a hazard to their waistline. Lunchtime on Saturdays Rebecca would have a different establishment cater for the staff. Some restaurants were better than others and Rebecca gave everyone in the vicinity a chance. Today was a favorite, Jim's BBQ, the sauce and sides were to kill for. After lunch, Claire reported to Rebecca that the next appointment didn't make it. Not because they didn't want to but because she passed away. Her cancer was too far gone, the family registered her in hopes she would be able to hang on till she was seen, but she died just that morning. This wasn't the first time something like this happened, it just hurt every time it did. Rebecca went to her office as she always would do in situations like this and called the family to express her condolences. Minutes later there's a knock on her office door, it's Claire. "Mrs. Marshal I have your next appointment ready," Claire says softly as she opens the door. Rebecca acknowledges with a nod and finishes up on the phone. Rebecca with a tear running down her cheek, hangs up and solemnly says, "Who do we have next?" Claire replies, "Mr. Dorian Johnson who is paralyzed from neck down. He's is in room 10." Rebecca takes a second to compose herself and fix her makeup then takes a deep breath and to herself says, "Just keep swimming, just keep swimming." She walks out of her office to attend to her next Fixee.

The rest of the day perks up and by her 2 pm appointment, Rebecca is back in her groove. "Claire who's next? Give me a tough one, love kicking sicknesses ass!" Rebecca says fired up. Claire briefs her on a boy with a spinal deformity. As they are walking to his exam room they pass by a television with the news on. They both look up at it to see a breaking story.

"We interrupt your regularly scheduled programming to bring you this breaking news. NASA is tracking an unidentified object moving at high velocity toward earth. The object was detected only moments ago as it was slowing down. It's being reported that the object is traveling at 1000000mph and decreasing. Hold on...It has just past the orbit of mars and will reach earth in minutes. NASA says International Space Station 2 has got a lock on the object and will send live video once they have a visual. One second... I think we have a visual of the object from the Space Station, yes we do..."

Rebecca watches intently, as the feed from space shows the craft getting larger as it encroaches upon the Station. The behemoth ship, which is 6000m in diameter, slows down to a crawl tracking alongside the space stations trajectory. Rebecca looks at the spacecraft, she can make out the familiar shape of the vessel...it's the Retaks spaceship. Rebecca screams out, "Holy Shit they're Here!!" Everyone in the building is now glued to the television. The reporter continues,

"NASA says they are trying to make contact with the U.F.O., to no avail. The craft seems to be just following along the International Space Station 2, orbiting only feet away. As you can see from the outside cameras on the I.S.S.2 the ship looks like a small moon, a dark black icosahedron with each triangle mirror finished. Our space station is dwarfed by this giant... oh wait something is happening. Oh My God! The ship just collided into the space station."

At this time NASA cuts the video feed and the reporter just goes on rambling about what just occurred. Rebecca mortified of what she saw runs into an empty exam room, shuts and locks the door. She reluctantly turns on the Television in the room to the news. Breathing heavily, she scuffles for her phone in her pocket and presses the call button. The phone rings "Hello Becca." Maggie answers. Rebecca says hysterically, "Mom they're here!! The Retaks they're here!!" "What dear... what are you talking about? Maggie says concerned. "Have you not been watching the news? Their ship just crashed into the space station. Mom, they're here to kill us like they did the Remaks. I need to talk to the Remaks now." Rebecca's thoughts are all over the place. Maggie replies, "We're in the garden, hold on I'm running into the house to turn on the T.V. right now." Maggie watches the multiscreen footage of the ship in space from the second orbiting Space Station, I.S.S.1. She's watching the live feed and also the replay of the collision being looped. Professor Lambkin walks in slowly behind her and gasps, "Oh my god they are here, aren't they?" The Retak's craft pilots closer into Earth's Thermosphere crashing into and destroying three satellites along the way. It then post itself in the southern hemisphere over the continent of Australia, tracking along with the earth's rotation. This is still all being broadcasted from Space Station 1, which has put some distance between them, orbiting high in the Exosphere. Suddenly a black ray shoots out from the craft, beaming down to the eastern part of Australia where the population is most dense. The news cuts to a live broadcasts in Sydney, the beam is a form of transport for the Retaks who are dropping in waves and instantly vaporizing everyone in sight, even the news crew filming. The television goes black. Rebecca's anxiety is at a high she tells her mom she'll call her back and hangs up. She goes and lays on the exam bed and starts breathing deeply trying to calm herself. It takes a few minutes but she's able to relax enough to go into a Trans dream state. Out of the darkness the Remaks appear, Rebecca horrified says, "The Retaks are here, what should I do?" They reply, "We were always afraid they would one day show up. You unlike us can fight, you must fight in order to survive." "But I saw the weapons they have, how are we to compete with that? They'll wipe out all of us in days. The Remaks pause then, "They are in physical form, which mean they are breathing earth's air, and therefore susceptible to your sicknesses and diseases. This environment will be the death of them." Rebecca confused replies, "You want me to give them a cold? I don't see how that would stop them." The Remaks reply, "Rebecca, you cannot be affected by disease but they can. You have to infect them all, that is your only hope. Your species must find a way, to save humankind and us. Rebecca wakes up out of the trance state to Quintin yelling at her, "Becca wake up, we gotta go now!!" He grabs her hand hurriedly dragging her off the bed and out of the room. Some people are still glued to watching the destruction transpiring on the news, others are fleeing. Quintin guides his wife out the back door into the parking lot where their car and driver sit waiting. They get in and the driver says, "Mrs. Marshall I have been ordered to stay on the premises and have you wait in the car for your safety, the helicopter is on the way." Rebecca replies, "My dad no doubt?" No sooner did her phone ring displaying an incoming call from her father. "Dad what are you doing?" She answers. "I have a chopper en route, the President and his staff want to meet with you. You are being flown to the White House, I'm flying there right now to accompany you." Trevor says. Just then, the Sikorsky RR lands 100ft away from the parked car. A two-man secret service detail emerge and run over to Rebecca's car. "Dad the chopper just landed," Rebecca says a little overwhelmed. "Good I'll see you in two hours, everything is gonna be alright, I love you, bye kiddo." "Bye dad, love you," she replies. Quintin helps Rebecca out of the car and the detail whisk them both onto the aircraft, in seconds they are in the air. Nervously Rebecca holds Quintin's hand as she sits quietly looking out the window. She sees lines of cars and people beginning to flock to grocery stores in a panic for supplies. People's fears are consuming them in the wake of seeing the invaders from space killing everything in sight. She squeezes his hand as a tear rolls down her face.

They arrived at a private heliport in D.C. where they are shuttled in an armored car to meet with the president. It was 4:25 pm when they entered the White House gates. As they get out of the car a redhead skinny black-suited twenty-five-year-old presidential aide greets them, "Hi my name is Gary; welcome to the White House Mrs. Marshall we are all fans of your work. Would you please come with me the president is waiting," Rebecca and Quintin are directed to a secured area in the White House, they enter the Situation Room where a company of high officials are seated around a giant round wood table chattering strategies. Trevor is also there sitting directly across from the President, there's one open seat next to him and he waves Rebecca over to sit next to him. She hurries over; the chattering subsides as everyone realizes who just entered the room. Rebecca oblivious of the looks, sits and whispers to her dad, "What am I doing here?" she then finally raises her head to see all the faces starring back at her, locking eyes with the Commander and Chief. Trevor whispers back, "You're here to tell us what to do." The President says, "Thank you Mrs. Marshall for accepting my invitation to meet with me. We know all about you and your capabilities, given the present situation I was hoping you could give us a suggestion on a way to defeat this alien threat." The room is so silent you could hear a pin drop. Rebecca is so nervous she can feel her body heating up and her hands are starting to sweat. It feels like an eternity Rebecca wants to say something, anything but nothing is coming out. An army general blurts out, "This is a waste of time she's one of them, she probably is the reason they're here. She brought them here." The round table erupts with arguments for and against Rebecca. All the while the President, a distinct middle-aged African-American woman, Harvard graduate from North Carolina, calmly sits looking at Rebecca waiting for a response. Finally, Rebecca slowly stands up and calmly says, "Madam President it's an honor to be here, in all this time I've never been to the White House, thank you for the invite.' The officials bickering immediately subsides. 'To address the gentlemen's comment, I did not bring them here nor did the Remaks, why would they. They fled their planet to avoid extermination from the Retaks. I have been dealing with people like you for years and there's just no reasoning. You believe I am a threat to your way of life when all I've been doing is giving people, a new life. I can only assume you called me here to help defeat the Retaks, and that's what I will try and do. The Retaks will not stop till we are all dead...the whole world is in for the fight for survival, we are all in this together." The President says, "Do you have an idea to defeating them." One of the officials barks out. "We can nuke them; bomb them back to where the hell they came from." President responds, "I'm not detonating nuclear weapons on American soil, not only will I kill innocent civilians, I'd make our country uninhabitable for generations.' She takes a deep breath, 'Though hate the idea as I may, I will reserve that for my absolute option." Rebecca says, "I agree with the general we should bomb them. On the flight here I was thinking about what the Remaks told me and a way that we could maybe destroy the Retaks.

And all I could think of is War of the Worlds, in the movie the aliens are killed out by our planet's bacteria. We could load our most lethal diseases and bacteria into bombs and explode them wherever they are. They are not accustomed to earth's environment so they will not last long." The President interrupts, "Wouldn't we also be exposing humans to the same diseases, we may kill the Retaks but we'd also kill millions of people also." Rebecca looks at her father then back to the President. Yea I thought of that too… the way to avoid that is… I'd have to find a way to touch everyone on the planet in order to protect them from the bombs." The table erupts again, some of the members are screaming out, "I'm not letting her touch me and infect me with some alien, fuck that I'll go down fighting." Some are saying, "How would that even be possible to touch everyone on the entire planet that's preposterous!" Rebecca looks down at the table then sits. The ongoing chatter keeps getting louder, then the President softly says, "Rebecca you're for real aren't you?" The chatter subsides again. She replies, "Yes Madam President I am." President asks, "So if you touched me I would never suffer from disease or sickness again?" Rebecca replies, "Yes that's true and you'd double your life span." "Oh yes can't forget that one." The President smiles and says. Rebecca still nervous quickly smiles back. Everyone is waiting to see what the President will say next then she says, "Would you be willing to come over here and touch me?" Instantly senior members of staff jump to their feet in protest, the President gestures them down. "Madam President it would be my honor but I must warn you of the effects. You will experience, um, how should I say this politely…a sort of orgasmic experience followed by drowsiness which will make you sleep from 4 hours to a day. While asleep, you will be introduced to the Remaks who will give you a sort of orientation in your dreams. After you wake your metamorphosis will have taken hold and you will be transformed. Whatever you were once good at you will be better, whatever you were once deficient in you will be replenished. All of their strengths none of their weaknesses… One last thing you will only be able to get pregnant every five years." President asks, "Why every five years?" "It's a Remaks thing, but it saves us from overpopulating since we are expected to live so much longer." Rebecca replies. The President ponders for a second and says, "I agree. Let's do it." Advisors swoop in immediately, they're fanatically whispering in the president's ears and vehemently trying to dissuade her from going through with it. Opponents of the decision threaten legal ramifications to Rebecca and the President, who shuns them by saying, "My body my choice. I believe Rebecca and I are willing to be the first in line to try and defeat this imminent threat to humankind. Lead by example, right?" She waves Rebecca over, turns her chair and sits in front of Rebecca. The President quickly asks, "Will this hurt?" Rebecca smile and responds, "Not one bit, quite the contrary." "Okay carry on…Oh, wait I would like you to stay here tonight. I want you here when I wake. Is that okay?" Rebecca checks in with Quintin and her dad and gets the thumbs up, she excitedly replies, "Hell yeh!" "Good I'll have the staff prepare some rooms and if you need anything, I'll have one of my aides assigned to you for the night… Okay, let's get on with it. What do you want me to do, do I just sit here?" President says. Rebecca replies, "Yes, I'm simply going to touch the top of your hand, it will all happen in an instant." The White House photographer who has been taking pictures this whole time positions himself to catch this momentous occurrence. Rebecca tells everyone to close their eyes due to the eminent light they were about to witness. No one but Rebecca's crew and the President and her aides takes heed. Rebecca then says, "Okay, you all wanna be like the Germans in Raiders of the Lost Ark, don't say I didn't warn ya." She closes her eyes and concentrates then it happens, the flash temporarily blinds the naysayers in the room. The President stiffens up and then belts out a loud scream followed by uncontrollable laughter. "Oh My God! That was amazing, that was the greatest feeling I've ever had." The President exclaims. She looks around to see all the officials rubbing their eyes. One of her aides says, "Ma'am I suggest you retire to your chambers." "I agree." Rebecca adds. The President is escorted out of the room as Gary enters and says to Rebecca, Trevor, and Quintin, "Will you please follow me." Rebecca looks back at the members still at the table, a few are giving her a glaring look of disgust, she just smiles, shakes her head, and walks out.

It was 6:15 pm, Gary suggested they eat at the White House, boasting that the world-renowned chef they had on the premises would blow their palette's mind. This was a no-brainer for Rebecca she instantly agreed. Gary then explained that from this moment forward Rebecca would be guarded to a level, second only to the president herself. The higher-ups have deemed Rebecca and her gift a Top-Priority. They felt she was the key to defeating the Retaks, Rebecca was not as optimistic but was ready to do all that was needed of her.

The dinner table was set for three guests with candles and 200yr old china, set on a white Egyptian silk tablecloth. First part of dinner was a Sashimi sampler followed by rib-eye steak with red wine and bone marrow sauce with a crisp salad and sweet potato fries. Dessert was sticky toffee pudding, it was a delight to the eyes and stomach. Rebecca felt like royalty, she ate the whole meal with a smile on her face looking back and forth to her dad and husband.

After dinner, Rebecca's escorted to a private room where she is met by a woman and two men. The woman calmly says, "Hi I am Mrs. Bishop the president's intelligence advisor and these are my two aides, Mr. Diaz and Mr. Ramsey. We want to see if you'd be willing to brainstorm with us on how we can possibly fulfill your idea. Is that okay with you?" Rebecca full and relaxed from the meal she just had, complies and calmly says, "I'm all ears." Mrs. Bishop says, "We've had our eyes on you for some time now. We've even spoken to a few of your past, how should I say your patients. The president has been extremely interested in you and your ability." Rebecca interrupts, "So the president asking to be touched randomly wasn't quite random at all I take it." "No not quite I'm afraid, I'm sorry if you thought that. She has wanted to have you here, to meet you in person for some time now, just wished it were under better circumstances." Mrs. Bishop replies. "Well let's stop wasting time, people are dying. What's your idea?" Rebecca says. Mrs. Bishop says. "Well okay…Mr. Diaz brought up a curious question." She looks toward her aide and Mr. Diaz says, "Is it possible for you to affect more than one person if they were touching another, say if you touched me while I was holding Mr. Ramsey's hand. Would your touch carry through to us both?" A few seconds of silence then fell as Rebecca's eye rolled randomly as she thought, then she said, "I don't know if never tried that before. Do you want to try and find out?" Mrs. Bishop smiles and says, "We were hoping you'd say that." She then leads Rebecca through a door on the other side of the room. The door opens to a large room occupied with a staff of medical workers, dressed in blue scrubs and dark shades, standing around two beds. "Did I even have a choice?" Rebecca snarly says. "You did, we were just prepared to do our best to convince you." Mrs. Bishop cautiously replies. The two aides then sit on two chairs that are facing each other in the middle of the room. Noticeably nervous they hold each other's hands, they both look at Rebecca and give the okay nod. Rebecca laughing says, "It's so funny how nervous people are before and then once it happens, all they want it to be back before it happened to do it again.' She winks at the two men, 'Okay everybody ready here we go…"

It's 1:45 am Sunday when Rebecca is woken by Gary whispering, "Mrs. Marshall please wake up the president is awake and wants to talk to you." Groggy she gets up and says, "What happened? The last thing I remember was I was gonna touch the two gentlemen. What happened did it work?" "Yes, ma'am it did, but you instantly passed out after. You've been out for five hours. The two men just woke up as well, Mr. Diaz had cancer and now he's cured. While you were asleep, they devised a plan that may work, the president wants to fill you in. I'll be right outside when you're ready." Gary replies. Rebecca looking around sees her husband in the bed next to her in what she would come to find out was Lincoln's Bedroom. Trying not to wake him she cleans herself up and heads out to meet with the president.

Rebecca is again taken to the Situation Room where this time she is seated right next to the president. The same officials are seated around the table but this time the looks are less hateful. The President says, "Rebecca I feel amazing the Remaks are wonderful, thank you again.' She nods to Rebecca, 'While you were sleeping my brilliant team came up with a plan to inoculate people on a mass scale. And the C.D.C. is working with the military to create an aerial disbursal bomb to deliver lethal doses of bacteria that we believe will stop the Retaks in their tracks. The only problem now is, do you know why you passed out after you touched Mr. Ramsey and Mr. Diaz?" Rebecca baffled shoulder shrugs and says, "I have no idea why I did, but the Remaks did tell me in my dream that this would work. Now how do I get the whole world to hold hands?" President Sanders leans in toward her and whispers, "Rosemary's Den."

Officials around the table go on to explain the operation "Rosemary's Den". Rebecca would be jetted city to city where local governments would have their citizens' round-up in gymnasiums, warehouses, indoor stadiums. Every participant would hold each other's hand forming a human chain, Rebecca would then complete the chain, creating a "Fixing" chain effect. A team of trained volunteers would be left to care for everyone in their sleep stage. And an explosives detail would be left behind with bombs strategically placed in preparation to defend against an invasion from the Retaks. Rebecca would then be sent to the closest ready city or town. This was the plan for America, tedious yet still effective with a projected completion of two months. Australia was doing their best to fend off the intruders, they were losing twenty men per Retak. They were given one month before they'd be 100% occupied. Other surrounding countries were reluctant to send in help for fear of not having the resources to protect their own country if invaded. Mass texts were sent to government leaders worldwide about Operation Rosemary's Den. America would send troops to fight and maybe slow down the advancing Retaks while Rebecca was inoculating the states and then Canada would be next followed by Mexico and South America. Rebecca in hearing all of this jumped up and ran to the bathroom to throw up. Dinner was now all in the toilet, she washes her mouth out and then hunches over the sink staring at herself in the mirror. "How am I supposed to do this…I don't know if I can do this." She says defeated. She solemnly goes out of the bathroom, and with a slow pace, she walks down the hall back to the Situation Room. On the walls of the hallway are past presidents' paintings along with quotes. She stops to read one said by the 26th President Theodore Roosevelt *Courage: "A soft, easy life is not worth living if it impairs the fiber of brain and heart and muscle. We must dare to be great; and we must realize that greatness is the fruit of toil and sacrifice and high courage… For us is the life of action, of strenuous performance of duty; let us live in the harness, striving mightily; let us rather run the risk of wearing out than rusting out."*

Rebecca knew what she had to do; she walks into the room and says, "Let's commence Operation Rosemary's Den."

chapter fifteen

CAANTACT

Australia fell on January 3, 2041, almost two months after the invasion. Almost all the citizens of the great nation were killed, out of a population of 30 million people, only 5 thousand remained. Scattered throughout the massive continent being a form of the rebel resistance. They were roughly 25000 Retaks occupying the land rummaging through everything they could find, destroying everything they did not need. They enslaved captured rebels and used them for sport hunting. One night over the cover of darkness the black icosahedron ship came to rest on the surface by Ayers Rock in central Australia. The rebels attempted to attack the mother ship with help from America and other foreign allies using missile strikes and ground forces, the outcome was not in the resistance's favor. All attacks were like future fights shown in the movie The Terminator. Earthlings were no match for the black behemoth, it would shoot out a black ray that would instantly vaporize any approaching threats. Australia was the Retaks stronghold now, they fortified all corners and then they started to look toward the next conquest. Their ship traveled north and deployed thousands of Retaks to overtake new countries. First was Papua New Guinea, which succumbed after two weeks as well as Indonesia and Malaysia. Vietnam resorted to past methods of tunnel dwelling, guerilla attacks, and booby traps. This lasted for a few weeks. The ratio of kills was 32 Vietnamese to one

Retak. All countries that had encountered the terrestrial nemesis had given all they could in trying to defeat this foreign enemy. But the sight of love ones and countrymen being vaporized to dust broke the strongest of fighters. The citizens are just not designed, nor prepared to fight such a powerful adversary, all of Southeast Asia fell with ease. China was the next target, their president decided their army was going to go with a different approach…victory or death.

It was now mid-March, you could see Rebecca was visibly pregnant, eight months to be exact. The timeline on fixing the citizens of the country was not going according to plan. Only half the country had been inoculated, corralling people proved more difficult than first described. There were a variety of individuals dissuading sects of people for reasons from religion to fear-mongering to straight-up saying it was a self-rights violation. The government filled the airways with PSA announcements informing that if invaded, Bio-Bombing was going to be a form of defense, and the only way to survive it would be to be inoculated with the Remaks. The wealthy were buying up underground bunkers in remote areas and running away to escape the carnage. The poor were looting and rushing country borders to escape the onslaught. The world was in chaos and misinformation filled the airways, some people even believed there was no such invasion, and it was all a government conspiracy. The Retaks had created the apocalypse.

Rebecca arrived in the incredibly famous Silicon Valley. She was tired as usual but still resilient with her efforts. She is escorted to a giant warehouse, where she sees five thousand people ready and waiting for her gift. There's a podium in front with a microphone ready for her to address the eagerly awaiting crowd. She takes a deep breath, smiles, and cheerfully greets the crowd with, "Good morning Silicon Valley, how are you all doing today, you guys ready for "The Feeling?"… Throughout time "The Touch" had gone through its series of renaming due to the younger generation, from "The Experience" to "The O" to "The Fix" it was currently called "The Feeling". Rebecca gives a detailed description of what everyone is due to experience and then has her team prepare everyone. After twenty minutes, all the sitting participants are hand locked in a human chain with the open link ready for Rebecca's contact. She fulfills her task to a deafening burst of five thousand people experiencing blissful glee. Her faint spells are now not an issue anymore. It still puts a smile on Rebeca's seeing the reactions people had after she was done with them. Rebecca is on a strict time schedule she waves to the jubilant crowd and is again escorted out of the warehouse. On the way to her awaiting car, two young men dressed in suits approach her and are immediately met with three guns drawn from her security detail. The men instantly throw their hands up in compliance and one says, "We mean you no harm Mrs. Marshall, can we please talk to you for one minute. I promise it'll be worth your while." Rebecca gestures to her team to stand down and says, "You got 59 seconds…go." Frantically the man pulls out his phone and says, "My name is Noah Caan, this is my brother Jake we created an App called Caantact that can transfer a person's touch from phone to phone. We developed a special haptic code that will connect someone's touch through the screen on anyone's phone all you need is to have the App installed. We believe that you can use this to instantly "Fix" everyone in the world at one time or at least large groups…they'd just need to have the App.' He pauses and looks at his brother then back to Rebecca, 'Oh, and a really large screen cause this would be the biggest Zoom call ever." Rebecca raises her eyebrow and smirks her lip. Noah quickly jumps in with, "Oh and to prove it works you can test it out with me and my brother right now, just take my phone and I'll take my brother's phone." He reaches out to hand Rebecca his phone, she leaves him hanging for a few seconds in disbelief. Slowly she extends and grabs the phone from the anxious creator. Noah says, "Awesome, okay my brother is gonna use the app to call you right now just answer." The phone rings and Rebecca answers, Noah and Jake are looking into their phone at Rebecca five feet away as she is just looking at them. Noah excitedly says, "Okay, my brother and I are going to touch the screen with our fingers all you have to do…I mean if you want to is touch yours and do what you do." The two men are awkwardly standing next to each other touching the screen in Jake's hand impatiently waiting for Rebecca to do her part. Rebecca looks slowly back and forward at the phone and the two men then say, "Here goes nothing." She closes her eyes touches the screen and instantaneously Jake's phone screen shines bright white, the men's eyes roll back in their heads and they fall backwards to the ground. Rebecca is amazed and shocked at the response. She goes to assist the men to their feet and says, "You guys ok? You fell back pretty hard." Noah in awe replies, "Freak yea, that was fucking amazing." Jake says, "That was incredible, I knew it would work Noah." Rebecca stands the men up and says, "We need to get this App to everyone ASAP. You men need to come with me, you'll be sleepy soon you can rest on the plane we have to go see the president right now.

Six hours later, Rebecca introduces Noah and Jake to President Sanders. It takes two days and forty I.T. people working nonstop to set up an official government site where the App could be accessed. Instructions were being broadcasted on every media outlet, from the internet to AM radio every half hour all day and night. Rebecca was set up with a giant wall IPad that was able to receive 10000 calls at one time. And every fifteen minutes she'd do a mass Touch inoculating people from all over the world. This was optimum seeing that she wasn't being hauled all over while being pregnant, she could be monitored in a controlled environment. That environment was also in a fortified underground undisclosed location code name "The Lair". Rebecca did not like being tucked away but for the safety of her baby, she was happy to be protected.

By late June China was on the losing side of the war. Their billion-man army had been cut to under 200000. They attempted a nuclear bomb strike it worked, but the damage it caused was irreversible and gave the reason that it should not be done again, it decimated everything and left the region inhabitable for years. Instead, they used Bio-Bombs on their population even though they had not all been inoculated, so along with Retaks their own people were dropping like flies. Unexpectedly the Retaks mothership lifted off from Central China and proceeded to head towards the North American continent. The movement of the giant ship is powerful and fierce, it was moving at 2000mph. The ship cruising at an altitude of ten thousand feet was like a traveling black hole. The Retaks would stop at any small island that was unfortunate to be in its path and annihilate the inhabitant. Hawaii because of the strong U.S. military presence there, gave a good fight. When U.S. intelligence noticed the Retaks were headed toward North America, the people of Hawaii swamped Rebecca. By the time the Retaks got to the Big, Island Bio-Bombs were wreaking havoc on the Retaks army, it was the first major blow to the Retaks, forcing them to change the strategy of their future attacks.

The ship arrived in the northern state of California on the morning of July 1st. The U.S. Forces threw everything it could short of nuclear, the ship withstood a barrage of fire and came out without a scratch on it. The previous night Rebecca had a visit from the Remaks. She hadn't really spoken to them in awhile even though she was always aware that they were there in the darkness of her sub consciousness. That night was special they came to her and told her that the baby was coming tomorrow. It was a happy moment for her, her life has been so hectic for so long she'd forgotten how peaceful it was to sit and just watch the ocean horizon of Zan. They also reminded her that she was The Light and the only real threat to the Retaks. She was the savior of the world and because of her, the people of earth had a chance. It was good to sit with her old friend they talked for a while then just sat in silence, it's what Rebecca needed.

The majority of the American continents and Europe, Asia and Africa had been inoculated via the app, with a few religious sects and anti-inoculators refusing to go along with the program. So when the Retaks ship came over California everyone thought no problem, we'll just wait for them to portal down and they'd bomb them to back to kingdom come. That plan was not to be, the Retaks changed their attack, and they expelled a thousand black balls 3ft in diameter that flew through the city of San Francisco blasting people with the same vaporizing weaponry. They were drones controlled by the crew inside the ship. It was more pleasurable for the Retaks to be on the ground killing everyone, but it wasn't mandatory. The drones would suffice for their objective.

While San Francisco was being decimated, Rebecca was giving birth. Her labor was quick she had the baby in 20 minutes and four hours later she was up and about like nothing happened. They named the baby girl Mary Hope Marshall-Williams. She was a cute baby quiet as can be. Quintin held his baby who looked normal except for the longer than average body and slightly oversized big brown eyes staring up at him. He recognized one thing, the nose, her nose was spot on for her daddy's nose. Rebecca smiled seeing her ever-supportive husband holding their child, Quintin had wanted this for so long. It made her happy that she could give him Mary. All this was short-lived intelligence officers and pentagon brass summoned Rebecca for a video meeting to find out how to combat this new threat. Bio-bombs were useless against drones. The ground troop's guns were effective at taking them out but the kill ratio was still 10:1, they were just too fast. The change in the attack plan made by the Retaks would be humanity's demise. As the big wigs again battled over a nuclear resolution. Rebecca spoke up saying, "I need a jet to take me to Flint ASAP, and I think I can end this now." Every one of the officials went quiet, President Sander softly says, "What's your plan, Rebecca?" Madam President I can't really go into this right now, I just need to see my brother... in the meantime, and if my plan fails I'll go along with whatever you all decide." "You have 24hrs that's all I can give you." the President says. Rebecca nods and hurries over kisses Quintin and her baby then hurries out as her detail follows behind her.

Its 8:35 pm by the time Rebecca lands in Flint, and 9:05 pm when she pulls up to her brother's restaurant. She enters the fine-dining eatery and asks the hostess where her brother is. She's directed to the kitchen, she finds Jordan head down busy preparing a beautifully colored meal on six plates. "I'll never stop being amazed by your talent." She says proudly. Jordan stops, looks up, and then back down, and says, "Well when you got it, it flaunt it right? What are you doing down here in the mud, thought you were up at the pentagon or something...' Jordan looks up again noticing his sister is no longer pregnant, and excitedly says, 'Oh Shit you had the baby!" He runs over to his sister and hugs her, "Where is it... girl, boy what did you have?" Rebecca laughing says, "It's a beautiful baby girl her name is Mary Hope Marshall-Williams. I'll bring her to come see you soon." "I'm an uncle holy cow I love it.' Jordan gasps, 'So what did you really come for?" Rebecca leans in and whispers in his ear, "I need you to use your amazing eyesight and find the orb tonight I have a helicopter waiting to take us to Caledonia Mines." Jordan looks back at his kitchen staff and says, "Julio finish this up for me I gotta go."

Jordan removes his apron and says to Rebecca, "Meet me in a half-hour mom's house." Jordan then exits out the back of the restaurant.

Rebecca gets to Maggie's place at 9:55pm and somehow Jordan is already there. She tells her detail to wait outside and walks into the front door. She sees Maggie, the professor and Jordan there sitting in the living room. Jordan has Uncle Pete's copper nugget in his hand. Rebecca confused says, "What's going on?" Jordan says, "The Orb is not in the Caledonia Mine." "Well we gotta find it and we need to find it now." Rebecca says with urgency. "Why do you need it?" Maggie says. "I'm going to use it to destroy the Retaks ship, I just know it'll work." Jordan gets up and says, "Follow me." Rebecca follows him by herself out the back door then he says, "About 10yrs ago I woke up and made it my mission to find the Orb. I figured I had the gift of sight who else should it be to find it like I was meant to. So I told mom what I was up to and not to tell you or anyone and I went off to find my white whale." Jordan stops walking at the garden which is the lushes garden Rebecca's ever seen. He then goes to the center of the garden and starts digging into the soft soil. "I went up to Caledonia Mine in the middle of summer, talk about humidity. I had supplies to last me a week and GPS and no clue where to start looking. The first day I just went to the highest hill, I figured I'd use my super vision to maybe see it glowing green…I didn't see shit." I roamed hopelessly for four days and found jack squat. At around noon on the fifth day, I came upon this enormous sycamore tree that had fallen recently. I remembered Uncle Pete said something about a big sycamore tree. I was thinking this has got to be it. I started digging around and moving dead leaves…nothing. Then I sat down on the tree trunk took a sip of water and noticed a patch of grass in this one area that was full and green as can be and I remembered the barn. I started moving the grass apart and pulling the dirt up and there it was.' Jordan has cleared about a foot of topsoil from the garden and Rebecca can see light starting to peer through. 'I had forgotten how beautiful the orb was and it was still pulsing green. I started digging around to loosen it up then I touched it and it stopped pulsing as if it knew me. I froze thinking maybe I did something wrong. I remember you said that Uncle Pete touched it and went to where he thought of… that was my plan. So I touched it again and it instantly turned red, I pulled back I couldn't think of where to send it. The barn was gone, the only place that kept popping in my head was mom's garden, so I said what the hell. I closed my eye thought of the garden and touched it. It rumbled turned bright red then shot up into the sky and disappeared. And when I came home it was exactly where it thought of." A couple more brushes of dirt and Rebecca sees the thing that changed her life pulsing red. "So here it is what are you gonna do with it?" Jordan asks. "I'm gonna save the fucking day." She says.

Rebecca woke up early the next day the Remaks came to her last night and told her the orb was hers to do as she pleased. She gets on the phone with the president and explains her plan. She was going to use the orb to destroy the Retaks ship. The orb was indestructible to a point she could guide like a missile and make Swiss cheese of their ship. The Retaks were still hovering over northern California tallying up deaths, Rebecca needed to get the orb there quick. After Rebecca hangs up with the president she goes to the garden, the orb stops pulsing and just holds bright red like it's ready for a command. She touches the orb and it turns purple she closes her eyes and commands the orb to rise out of the ground and hover in place. The orb rumbles and lifts out of the garden coming to rest at eye level with her. Rebecca seeing the full size of the orb up close pointing at her, backs up a little and the orb moves with her. Even though it's only the size of a large T.V. it's still intimidating to her. She reaches out and pushes the giant teardrop down to her waist level so it's not in her face. The orb stays, she walks forward and it follows her like a puppy dog. She chuckles, she then looks out to the tree line about a thousand feet away and points to it, immediately the orb shoots over in blazing speed. She then puts her hand down to her side and one second later the orb is right there. She laughingly says, "Wow I have my own pet orb."

Rebecca gets her security detail to acquire a cargo van so she can transport the orb. Time is of the essence she says bye to her mom and promises to bring Mary by soon. Rebecca gets into the cargo van having the orb hover in the bay just behind her passenger seat. The shiny solid purple orb has taken on a matte finish now; it stands at the ready on the ride to the airport. Rebecca uses this time to

FaceTime Quintin and Mary, it had only been a day but she felt she had not seen them in a week.

At the airport a C-17 Globemaster III is used to haul the orb to California, it takes 5hrs to land just outside San Francisco where the army set up a command center in a fortified cave in the hills. The once-great city is covered by the ocean marine layer, the thick fog hugs the smoldering buildings. The military has resorted to evacuating the civilians in the city and just bombing anywhere they see drone activity. The effort makes little damage seeing that once the number of drones drops the mothership releases more to continue the reign of carnage. Suddenly the ship starts moving in Rebecca's direction. She points to the ship the orb shoots directly towards the center of the colossal ship. The military and Rebecca watch in wonderment as the orb rips a hole through and through the black monster. Cheers cry out as you can hear a whirring sound shriek from the mothership. The Retaks retaliate with a swarm of fresh drones headed towards Rebecca. She has the orb strike again and again each blow crippling the spacecraft. The military are firing away and using sound waves to destroy the incoming drones to defend Rebecca's assault. The mothership cannot take any more hits from the crystal missile, it retreats at an incredible speed high up into the atmosphere. Its outside of Rebecca's sight she can't attack it with the orb anymore. "Fuck!" she screams out. Rebecca sulks down onto the dirt the orb undamaged returns to her side. She looks up to the sky with a feeling of defeat, she was so sure this would work. Within 2hrs, the military with heavy losses, defeat the wave drones and for the first time in months, earth is not under attack. The international space station reports that the ship is back orbiting in the Thermosphere and looks like the Retaks are making repairs. A colonel walks up to Rebecca hands her a phone and says, "The president is on the phone for you." Rebecca takes the phone begrudgingly, "Madam President." "I'm assuming that is not the way you planned this offensive, but we are grateful that you got them to retreat..." The president says. Rebecca replies, "No Ma'am, but the break-in fighting is good." "What do you suggest we do now? Because they're up there fixing their ship and planning another attack and I'm sure this next one will be worse than the last." President Sanders replies. Rebecca answers, "We cannot allow them to reenter. Ma'am we have to take the fight to them." President snarky replies, "Well I don't know how we're supposed to go about that, anything that we send up there they'd blast out of the sky or just speed away... space is their turf." "Ma'am I know what I must do, give me a half-hour." Rebecca replies and hangs up on the president. Rebecca then goes into the cave to the communications specialist, she asks her to connect her via video to her family ASAP. The wiz kid within seconds calls up Rebecca's husband, mom, dad, brother, and uncle. Rebecca adds, "Oh I need you to add in Beverly Charleston." "Yes, ma'am one sec." Moments later everyone that means anything to her is looking at her via video. Rebecca opens with, "We gotta do this more often.' She smiles, 'Hi mom, Hi Bev, Hi Uncle, Hi dad, Hi Jordan, Hi Babe, Hi little Mary.' Her smile slowly disappears, 'I have some bad news the plan I had did not work. The Retaks escaped into space, we believe if they come back to the surface, they will be even more ruthless than before. We have to take the fight to them, in space... well more so, I do. That's why I'm calling I have to take the orb." Quintin interrupts, "What are you saying? How are you taking the orb into space Becca, what are you saying?" Rebecca sadly replies, "You all know what I'm saying, it's the only way. Too many people have already died, there will not be another if I can help it." Just then the Colonel walks into the cave and excitedly says, "They're on the move again they're coming back." Rebecca takes a deep breath as tears roll down her face, everyone on the screen is crying except for Mary. Rebecca notices that and tells Quintin to hold her up so she can get a better look. Mary's smile and big brown eyes are infectious. Rebecca says, "I still can't believe you came out of me, I was told that I was the one. Untrue you, you my precious princess you are the one. I love you.' Rebecca backs up and looks at each one of them, 'I love all of you, you made all of this worth doing. I have to go... I love you so much." A wave of voices cry out to not go, Rebecca can't take it she tells the specialist to please hang up, reluctantly she does and the cave goes quiet. Rebecca wipes the tears away from her eyes and takes a deep breath the looks to the colonel and says, "Tell the president there's nothing to fear anymore." Rebecca turns to the orb that has been there at her side the whole time, "I guess deep down inside I knew this is the way it had to be. You've always been a part of me, now it's time for me to be part of you... We win Gracie." Rebecca closes her eyes, her white aura emanates bright like the sun, lighting up the cave, her mortal body drops to the floor. All who are in the cave are stricken in awe, it's like a heavenly angel. Rebecca's aura then bonds with the orb, it's no longer purple but bright white. It then flies out the cave hurtling towards the colossal evil breaching its way back to earth's floor. Rebecca now in her higher essence feels each of the Remaks that has chosen her for this journey for the preservation of life. The Retaks cannot defensively react in time, the orb spears the spaceship putting an enormous hole on its hull, then comes to a stop in the center of the beast. The Remaks and Rebecca are one, the orb starts to rumble vigorously and begins to fracture, light starts emitting through the cracks. Retaks try to fire upon this imminent doom but it's too late, the orb explodes with such force it rips the giant ship into smithereens and all the Retaks within it.

July 10, 2041

It was a beautiful summer day, not too hot, not too humid, it's just a perfect morning at Uncle Ed's church. This is a day no one ever thought would ever come to be. Jordan, though devastated, stands tall on behalf of his sister. He gave the broadcasted eulogy to a worldwide audience, he started with, "The Remaks said that Rebecca would save everyone and bring the world together, and they were right. In life she gave people a better life, now in death she has made the world a better place to live. She would be happy to know she meant this much to everyone, but she'd be ecstatic knowing everyone meant that much to each other. She had a touch that healed and now the world is healed and through her sacrifice, humankind will endure and blossom, guaranteeing a future for generations. She was my sister, my best friend and though I miss her, she's not gone, far from it. Rebecca is a part of us all for eternity, so go forth and shine your white light bright.

THE END

CPSIA information can be obtained
at www.ICGtesting.com
Printed in the USA
BVHW031329200922
647492BV00012B/944

9 781958 030769